Lie Down with Silk and Daggers

From the Jazz Malone series

Frank Walters Clark

PROLOGUE

The tires protested when he jammed the brakes and turned, careening off the asphalt road and onto a sandy two-track that led through giant cypress trees to a clearing by the lake. His mouth was dry and his hands felt sticky. His heart was pounding as he slid to a stop and killed the engine. He flung open the door, banging it against its hinge stops. Tom Petty crooned, "It's Good To Be King" on the radio, but the ringing in his ears distorted the familiar words.

The thick, humid air made rivulets of sweat torture his eyes. He grabbed the wadded, sea green silk dress off the seat and climbed out. Stumbling through the gate, he went down the sandy embankment to the lake and stared at the glassy surface. Images crowded his mind: her softly glowing bedroom lamp, her velvet skin, and her screams. He waded into the tea-colored water and turned back the folds of the crumpled dress.

The fabric was spattered and torn and had blotted the stains off the sharp blade that lay hidden there. The dagger seemed hot in his hand, and he threw it as far as he could. The polished surfaces glistened as it rolled and turned, arcing in the late afternoon sun, before falling into the lake.

He held the dress to his face. Her perfume lingered, mixed with her essence on the cloth. He could hear her throaty laugh and feel the warmth of her embrace, her body moving lithely beneath him.

Then the nightmare began again. Another man, his arms around her, their lips pressed together, her fingers caressing his face. The memory was like acid in his brain, burning away feelings, corroding his emotions.

He churned the dress in the watery gloom and the stains slowly bled away. All traces of her were gone. His legs made eddies as he dragged the dress back to the shore. It fluttered with a life of its own, like a butterfly intoxicated by nectar.

Among the cattails on the embankment, he found a limestone rock and laid it inside the dress. He rolled it up and knotted the long, widow's lace sleeves tightly around it. He pressed the cold fabric to his lips, then threw the bundle out over the lake and it dropped into the awaiting waters.

Goodbye, my love, he whispered. *Now you are forever mine.*

Disturbed by the splash, a snowy egret winged its way across the grotto. Ripples floated silently across the lake and washed onto the beach.

He sat among cypress knees listening to cicadas offering a song to the sun. Purple thunderheads gathered over the far reaches of the Gulf of Mexico. Lightning danced in the distance between towering clouds and blue-black waters, summoning angels to bear witness to his deeds. The wail of sirens came from afar.

The first night they had visited this hideaway the moon was full and the shadows deep. For a man his age her young body was a cool oasis, a refuge from the consuming fires of his everyday world.

No one would find him here, in this place of silk and daggers. It was a place where they had played, a place of limitless passions. But there was no escaping his compulsion. No cure for his ache of the heart, his sickness, the wasting away of his soul.

1

In the pre-dawn stillness of a tropical July, the bruised and swollen skies blanketing Tampa Bay unleashed their furies. By seven a.m. the storm had run its course and the temperature had risen to a rheumy seventy-five degrees. The well-scrubbed, heavy air draped itself over the lazy sprawl of St. Petersburg.

Jasper Malone was just finishing his morning walk with his bull terrier, Redford, his Buccaneer's

t-shirt wet with exertion. The skies had cleared and the sun glistened on streets and sidewalks.

After cleaning up and dressing, Malone sat at his desk with a mug of hot coffee and the St. Peters-burg Times. As he was reading the classifieds, the phone warbled.

Lifting the receiver, he said, "Malone and Associates."

"Jasper Malone, please?" a feminine voice said.

"Speaking."

"This is Anne Hurt," she said, "with Mr. Amato's office? He would like to meet with you at your earliest convenience. Would next Tuesday morning be possible?"

"What is this concerning, Ms. Hurt?"

"The whereabouts of Mrs. Esther Hunter."

"Tuesday will be fine, Ms. Hurt," Malone said, intrigued by the possibility of another case.

Private investigations and fiction writing made up the bulk of Malone's day, with small-scale importing of Mayan Indian goods filling the gaps. He was satisfied with the independence his work afforded.

* * *

Malone swam in the cool waters of Tampa Bay that afternoon, near the inverted pyramid of the St. Petersburg Pier. The white sands and sparkling waters of the North Shore beaches were a short bike ride from his condo overlooking Mirror Lake.

While Redford frolicked along water's edge, chasing fiddler crabs, Malone marked laps up and down in the water just off the beachfront. The impending visit to Tony's office weighed heavily on his mind. So many things had changed, and revisiting memories from his youth was often a mixed bag of pain and pleasure.

Anthony Amato was his boyhood friend, and if the need arose, his legal counsel. They had grown up together around Lealman, a neighborhood lying on the northern borders of St. Petersburg. As boys they played baseball on sandy lots prickling with sand spurs and stick-tights, and often swam in the small lakes that dotted the neighborhood.

Tony had studied law at nearby Stetson College. A couple of hard years in the public defender's offices brought an offer from one of Florida's most visible and busiest law firms, Baxter, Brannon and Moss. Five years later, he was given a full partnership.

Back at the condo Malone showered, his thoughts turning to the Hunter family. Images of the elderly couple were among the few fond memories Malone had of his

youth. The Black Cow root beer floats Esther had made.
A beautifully tooled, foot-pump organ that belched musty
air when she played it. Faded daguerreotypes from the
Big One that Harold would bring out, soldiers long dead
but fighting on in the old man's memories.

Clean and shaved, Malone donned Levi's, Reeboks
and a Hawaiian print shirt, then loaded Redford into his
Chevy four-by-four. East bound traffic slowed to a crawl
on Howard Franklin Bridge, as it often did during
morning rush hour.

Malone quickly navigated the towering canyons and
busy streets that crisscrossed downtown Tampa. After
checking all the lower levels of the parking garage and
finding nothing, Malone got lucky at the top.

A stunning strawberry-blond was backing a forest-
green, T-top Porsche 911 out of a slot. A pair of retro-
sixties, Foster-Grant sunglasses, hid her eyes and she was
wearing damask-red lipstick.

With a smile playing at the corners of her lips, she
mouthed the words "nice dog," then waved as she pulled
away. Malone bleeped his horn, then laughed when he
read her neon-framed license plate: LEG'L ASS'T.

After locking Redford's harness to the truck's roll-
bar and pouring him a bowl of water from a gallon jug,
Malone jaywalked Tampa's busy Franklin Street.
Boarding the outside glass elevator of Compton Towers
South, he rode to the thirty-eighth floor and Tony's
office.

Baxter, Brannon, Moss and Amato's waiting room
was modern luxury. Plush mauve carpeting, lumbering,
black-mahogany side tables and intricately-carved and
richly upholstered Queen Anne chairs. Expensive
paintings were hung for viewing at strategic locations.

The decor seemed ostentatious to Malone.

"Tony will be right with you, Jazz," Mrs. McVee said. "Would you like a coffee?"

"Thank-you, yes, Mrs. McVee," he said, sinking into one of the plush chairs as she hurried off.

Prim and proper, Ellen McVee had logged over forty years with the firm, and knew a great deal about the plodding entanglements of law. More in fact than most of the war horses frequenting Compton Towers or the privileged judicial chambers standing next door in the tower's imposing shadow.

The coffee was delicious. Sweetened with brown sugar and seasoned with just a hint of orange, it had a wonderful aroma.

"I have measured out my life with coffee spoons..." Mrs. McVee smiled.

"T.S. Elliot, if I'm not mistaken," Malone said. "As of late, so have I."

"I know exactly what he meant," she said.

Tony emerged from his inner sanctum. He was impeccably dressed; wearing a tailored, blue linen shirt, matching tie and suspenders, and dark-blue pleated, pinstriped pants. He had the old world bearing of a man who traded admiring glances with beautiful women.

"Howzit, compadre?" Malone grinned. "It's been a while."

"Come on in, Jazz," Tony said. "Hold my calls please, Ellen. When Anne gets back, send her in." He turned and walked into his office and Malone followed.

"Have a seat," Tony said, closing the door. "This is a relatively simple matter, but Anne will give you the details when she gets back."

Malone lowered himself into a stuffed, burgundy

chair at one corner of an imposing black-mahogany desk. Typically effusive, it was unusual for Tony to pass off on the details. Malone felt an awkward tension in the room.

Tony plopped down and opened the top folder from a stack at one corner of his desk. He looked restless and unsettled as he flipped through the contents.

"Do you remember Harold and Esther Hunter," he said, "from First Baptist Church?"

"Sure," Malone said. "He sang baritone in the choir. Retired from federal service. She has the talk show."

"They've been good friends of my family for a long time."

"She used to baby sit my brother and me," Malone said, "when my mom went back to work at Graham's photo studio."

"Mr. Hunter passed away this past April," Tony said. "He was a life-long smoker and it caught up to him."

He stood and leaned against the floor-to-ceiling window, gazing at some object in the distance. Lost in thought for a moment, he turned and handed Malone the folder.

"They live in an old ramshackle place on some acreage over in Pasco County. North of Tarpon Springs."

There were several pictures of the Hunters taken at their anniversary celebration. A fifty-year banner hung in the background; one of Tony, standing between the Hunters. A couple of hand-written notes addressed to Tony and signed by Mrs. Hunter.

"So what do you need?" Malone said, scanning the notes.

"Mrs. Hunter recently came into possession of a very rare, Mayan sacrificial dagger. Technically it belongs to a group of foreign investors. A client of mine—John Tanner—is their American liaison. He's asked me to get it back and we would like you to locate it—and Mrs. Hunter, of course."

"I'll need a grand to go and one-fifty a day. Another grand, if and when I find the dagger—and her, of course."

"That's fine. We're offering an additional five-thousand-dollar bonus for successfully locating and retrieving the dagger. Privacy issues require no outsourcing and no publicity."

"I can handle that."

There was a knock at Tony's office door, and the most hauntingly beautiful women Malone had ever seen walked in. She had graceful curves and flawless skin. With honey-colored eyes and long, strawberry-blond hair, she seemed almost gossamer. She wore a black, two-piece suit, a bone-white blouse and spike heels. Her tangy perfume was like ambrosia.

"You must be Mr. Malone," she said, offering her hand. "I've been looking forward to meeting you. I'm Anne Hurt."

Her touch was electrifying. Too long absent from the mysteries of feminine influence, long dead fires roared to life deep inside Malone.

"Call me Jazz," he said, grinning weakly when he noticed Tony glance his way derisively.

"I'm sorry to interrupt," Anne said, sitting in the matching chair by Tony's desk and crossing long, elegant legs. "Kate Simons just called, Tony. Judge Bryant is expecting you in his chambers for the Keswick pretrial."

"Oh, hell!" he said, rising to leave. "I'd better go. Judge Bryant is a stickler about latecomers."

"No sweat, T-bone," Malone said. "Asta luego."

"Anne, will you bring Jazz up to speed on the Hunter case?" Tony said, pausing at the door. He pointed his fingers pistol-style at Anne.

"Will I see you later?" she asked. "At Michaels?"

"Eight o'clock," Tony said. "Can you make it, Jazz?"

"Like to, but I have to get home and feed my hound. I'll take a rain check, though."

"Give Redford a pat for me." Tony said as he left.

Anne began relating the Hunters' recent activities to him. Malone already knew much of the material, but he was mesmerized by her presence.

Better known by her stage name of Aunty Q, Esther Hunter had nearly a half-century of radio operations under her belt. She started out in San Francisco as an amateur, a "ham," with the call sign, K6OCJ. For a number of years now she had been doing a radio talk show on WUSF-FM, in Tampa. Live interviews and on-air readings from her collections of antiques reference books had become a Saturday afternoon tradition with many of her Tampa Bay listeners.

Malone found it difficult to concentrate. Anne was stunning and mysterious, a knockout combination for any man.

Stay away, the whispers in the back of his mind said. He knew that, given time and opportunity, Anne Hurt could easily become an obsession.

"Call me," Anne said later, touching his hand and handing him one of her business cards. "My home number is on the back."

Malone threw a coin in the fountain outside Compton Towers, feeling like a boy who's just discovered that girls have different parts. He remembered W.B. Yeats' line from The Secret Rose: "*A woman of so shining loveliness / That men threshed corn at midnight by a tress.*"

2

On the highway just north of the Greek sponge-fishing town of Tarpon Springs, Malone switched off the engine and rolled to a stop at the end Mrs. Hunter's driveway. First light crept through the Spanish moss-laden, sprawling branches of old oak trees embracing the house. Copper colored needles blanketed the ground around the tall and stately slash pines.

Draped in shadows, the old craftsman-style, two-story farmhouse was clad with well-weathered cedar-shakes. The porch light cast an umbrella of pallid light over the walkway. Hibiscus and azalea grew in clusters under the windows, and scratched at the siding in a soft breeze laden with Confederate jasmine.

Redford stood up on the seat and growled soft and low. His whole body quivered, and he was posturing, wanting to get out.

"Lay down," Malone told him, "or you don't do stud service Saturday."

A trellis arched over the walkway, bowing under the weight of a mass of red and white climbing roses, their velveteen bouquet permeating the air. Malone walked up on the wide-apron porch, then looked back at the truck.

Redford had sat back up on the seat and was peeking over the dashboard. Malone gave him the down sign and heard him grouch once, then disappear again.

Mrs. Hunter's front door had a bas-relief, inverted cornucopia on its exterior, the various fruits spilling out to the bottom edge of the door. Malone knocked and the thick door groaned as it swung open several inches.

"Mrs. Hunter?" he called through the gap. "Aunty Q?"

Malone called several more times, then pushed the door wide open. The living room had the heavy, wet odor of must and mildew. He groped along the wall, flipped on a light switch, and was shocked by what he saw.

Rare antiques, lamps, crystals—things that had taken the Hunters years to collect—had been trashed. Pictures were ripped and tilted at crazy angles, the glass smashed and peppered across the carpets. Wads of batting spilled out of a gutted, camel-back sofa that sat facing the fireplace.

A steady stream of water poured through a crack in the ceiling and rained from the pink-glass, chandelier. The Persian carpets were soaked, and a maze of water seeped over the black and white checkerboard tiles in the kitchen and trickled out beneath the back door. Every room on the first floor was a similar scene of carnage.

Water streamed down the stairs as Malone climbed to the second floor. Bedding had been scattered, mattresses sliced, and drapes ripped. Shredded towels had been thrown in the overflowing bathtub along with soap bars and toilet paper.

Whoever this imbecile had been, Malone thought, wreaking havoc on the ground floor had not been enough.

He shut off the water in the tub and walked downstairs. Shards of glass crunched wetly under his boots in the kitchen, and at the back door, the wall phone rang.

"Hunter residence," he said.

Next to the phone was a cork bulletin board, plastered with the dross elderly women are prone to collect: Notes, clippings, schedules and menus. Grocery lists, he noted, dating back several years, were tucked into niches.

"Did you find it?" a soft-spoken, male voice asked.

The phone went dead when Malone asked who it was.

Malone punched up 911 on his cell phone as he walked to his truck. He reported the details to a Pinellas County Sheriff's dispatcher, then sat back to await their arrival.

WUSF-FM was airing Vivaldi's Four Seasons when he turned on the radio. Reddy chased a gray squirrel up a pine tree, then whined while it danced just out of reach. Rays of light played tag with shadows between the spindled branches red-berried Cuban hollies, and the sun rose up over a robin's egg blue sky.

* * *

The Pinellas County Sheriff's crime-scene crew got right to the business of dusting the place, taking pictures and logging the evidence. A deputy at the head of the driveway lifted the crime-scene tape and waved an unmarked car through to the driveway at the end of the Hunters' ballistered porch.

A detective got out, scowling as he stretched his tall, muscular frame to full height. His square-jawed face belayed any interest in the crime scene crew's findings as he made a beeline up the porch stairs and over to the swing where Malone sat.

He was wearing a blue, sear-sucker suit that fit comfortably, and had his white hair buzzed off in a flattop. The motorcycle boots he wore had the high gloss shine of a black, Steinway grand.

Boots excepted, Malone thought, the man could have been at the helm of some corporate machine, rather than the rudder of a sheriff's skiff.

"What are you doing here, Malone?" he asked, pulling a thin cheroot from his lapel pocket. He bit the end off, spit it over the railing, then struck a match and lit the cigar.

Another of Malone's boyhood friends, Detective Lieutenant Vernon Cobb and his family had also made their home in the Lealman neighborhood. Dyed-in-the-wool Southern Baptists, George and Margaret Cobb did not believe in sparing the rod. Young Vernon often showed up for junior and senior high school gym classes with his back, buttocks, and legs covered in welts and bruises. Most were the shape of a two-inch wide belt with an oval-shaped buckle.

"I assumed you already knew why, Vern."

"Humor me," he said, eagle-eyed.

Malone remembered that, when Vernon Cobb had studied law enforcement at St. Petersburg Junior College, he had vied for the pistol marksman championship. His name eventually was engraved on the first-place trophy and he had missed very few things since.

"Like I told the deputy that took my statement," Malone said, "Tony asked me to check a few things about Mrs. Hunter."

"Just so you and Mr. Amato understand," Lt. Cobb said, easing into a voice of authority. "You see that tape?

This is now an official crime scene. No thing and no one goes in or out of this house without my say so. School chums not-withstanding."

"Fair enough, chief," Malone said, sensing that if he didn't leave immediately, things would get ugly. "I don't like the routine, though. Too militant for my liking."

The primary directive in the Cover Your Ass handbook every officer of the law owns—that an unused power moment is an opportunity squandered—had not escaped Lt. Cobb.

"Don't like the…listen, wise-ass," he said, clapping a big hand on Malone's shoulder and spinning him around.

"You don't want to do that," Malone urged, glancing over at the truck. Redford had pushed his head out the driver's window and was looking their way, snorting rapidly, testing the air and growling continuously in a low rumble.

"Are you refusing to cooperate with me?" Lt. Cobb said, tilting his head to one side and squinting at Malone.

"No, Vern. You just don't want to put your hand on me right at the moment."

Lt. Cobb gave Malone a deadpan look and turned to a specialist retrieving prints from the front door knob. "Andrews," he said, "make note of the fact a civilian named Jasper Malone has been advised regarding the Sheriff's Department crime scene s.o.ps relative to the Hunter investigation."

Andrews nodded indifferently. Then came the ominous sounds of Red's toenails clicking on the truck's windowsill, the soft thump of his landing, and then him galloping across the Hunters' front yard.

"Vern…."

Lt. Cobb's eyes went wide and his cigar dropped to the floor. His hand scrambled for his hip holster just as a fawn-colored blur flew in from the side. Redford had launched himself off the porch swing, and with the momentum knocked the detective flat on his back on the faded and worn planks of the porch.

Red stood over Cobb with his teeth chattering nervously, one paw on the lieutenant's chest like a wolf guarding its kill. Saliva began dribbling from the edges of his mouth onto the detective's neatly pressed suit.

"Get-this-mutt-off-me!" Lt. Cobb said through gritted teeth.

"Excuse me?" Malone said. "I don't think Reddy likes you impugning his blue-blooded ancestry that way, Vern."

"Just get him off me."

"Heel, Reddy," Malone commanded.

Lt. Cobb sat up, trying to preserve a degree of dignity.

"Get out of here, before I run you in for obstruction," Lt. Cobb said, standing up and brushing himself off. He pulled out a white linen handkerchief and dabbed at the splotches on his suit. "And get my permission before you come out here again. You hear me, boy?"

"You got it—Vernon," Malone said, starting for his truck. Redford ran ahead and waited at the driver's side.

Lt. Cobb hated it when anyone called him by his given name, but there was no love lost between the deputy and Malone. The man had expended far too much psychic energy growing up, Malone thought, trying to overcome his perceived humiliation of having the name Vernon. Never realizing he was hoisting himself on his own petard.

Malone backed out of Mrs. Esther Hunter's yard and turned onto the highway. Directly across the two-lane road from the property, pulled deep into the wooded undergrowth, was an eighties' vintage, four-door Plymouth. It had bronze-tinted windows and blue paint faded to a chalky film, and the splash panels were pocked with rust along the bottom. Spurs of light glinted off the driver's mirrored sunglasses.

Malone headed south on the shimmering asphalt road. The morning clouds had drifted away, leaving the sky a pale wash of daffodil. Brooks and Dunn's version of "My Maria" played on the radio.

The blue Plymouth was suddenly alongside the truck. Holding the steering wheel with one hand, the driver had slid over to the passenger's side of the seat, holding his left foot on the accelerator. He was trying to steady the magnum he had pointed at Malone.

Malone simultaneously down shifted and slammed on the brakes, and felt the shock wave when the guy's cannon went off. The slug barely missed his skull, blowing past and shattering the old truck's brittle windshield.

The Plymouth swerved and sideswiped Malone, then raced off down the highway. Huge, black arcs from the truck's tires were burned in a jagged line down the side.

Malone skewed wildly off the road onto the shoulder. The truck spun around in a complete three-hundred-and-sixty-degree circle and came to a stop in a cloud of dust, flying glass and ricocheting gravel.

He was trembling as he shut off the motor, and laid his head on the steering wheel. There was glass everywhere. The sudden stop had thrown Redford on the floor, where he lay quivering. Malone reached down to comfort him.

"It's okay, Reddy," he said quietly. "It's all over."

He called the Sheriff's Department and asked the desk sergeant to relay a message to Vern. Why had he been attacked and who was the man in the Plymouth? A lot of things didn't make sense in the world anymore, and this incident was right up there at the top of the list.

* * *

Malone sat on the tailgate and picked slivers of windshield glass off his arms and Red's coat. Lt. Cobb pulled up behind the truck with all his emergency lights flashing. Donning a tan Stetson, Cobb leaned against the fender of the unmarked white Caprice for a moment, then crossed his arms, eyeing Malone. He looked gritty and uncompromising.

'Can't keep your boots out of the cow dip, can you?" he called, walking over to Malone's truck. "Suppose you tell me what happened."

"Some wild card took a shot at me, Vern," Malone said. "The guy was watching the Hunters' place and followed me out. Tried to aerate my person with his chrome-plated cannon."

"And didn't come back to mop up, huh? You couldn't have been too important to him if he didn't come back and finish it."

"Maybe he was late for a doctor's appointment! How the hell am I supposed to know what that asshole was thinking?"

"Don't get hinky with me, boy," Lt. Cobb snapped. "If you want my help, just ask. If you want to do comedy, go see a barkeep at BayWalk or the Pier."

Lt. Cobb walked back to his car and stopped.

"You know where to find me. Meantime, get this piece of shit off the highway."

"You going to write this up?" Malone yelled, sliding down off the tailgate.

Lt. Cobb was annoyed. "Write what up? Big bird drops a big brick and blows out your stinking windshield? I call that a waste of my time and taxpayer dollars."

Twice in one day, Malone realized, he had violated a corollary of the Cover Your Ass handbook: never piss off people whose help you may need at some critical moment.

* * *

Triple-A towed his truck to Central Garage in St. Pete, and Malone had a taxi drop him and Reddy at the Tampa studios of WUSF-FM. He secured Redford to a jungle of root-runners hanging from a nearby banyan tree.

"Stay out of the dirt," he told him.

Redford looked at him dolefully and snorted. Walking out to the full length of the leash, he plopped down in a patch of black loam, then rolled on his back and dug his paws in the air.

Wonderful, Malone thought. Man's best friend. Giving me the canine equivalent of the finger.

The radio station was a concrete monolith two stories tall. The lobby had stainless-steel wraparound railings encircling the upper level of its spacious, atrium-style interior. The smell of new plaster and wet paint hung heavy in the air, and signs posted all around read, 'Please excuse our mess!'

Malone was the only one standing at the counter in the lobby, but waited patiently while the receptionist went on filing her fingernails. She finally turned around and peered at him over the top of fifties-style, red reading glasses, all the while never missing a stroke with her nail file. In Malone's mind she had instantly qualified for a cryonics research grant.

"Yes," she said, obviously bored. "Can I help you?"

"I'm looking for Barry Jensen," he said. "Your program director?"

She gave him another freezer blast. "I know who Mr. Jensen is. The question is who are you?"

He had often wondered where people like this took business classes and what had become of civil behavior in society. Maybe her rudeness could be attributed to breathing the head-spinning paint fumes all day.

"Jasper Malone," he said brightly. "Barry's expecting me."

"That remains to be seen." She spun around in her chair and punched a couple numbers on a PBX console. "I'll see if he's available. Take a seat."

An hour later, after reading a year-old copy of Good Housekeeping three times from cover to cover, Malone heard the receptionist clear her throat. The ice-queen was gesturing at the double doors leading to the radio station's inner sanctum.

He found Barry Jensen sitting in a little cubbyhole of an office near the end of the hall. The walls were covered with Beethoven and Mozart posters, and Jensen's desk was a jumble of computer, compact discs, programming logs, and music lists.

A short, fat man with dirty-blond hair cut pageboy style, Jensen was devouring a huge hamburger. As he mindlessly glutted, the burger dribbled a liquefied ketchup and mayonnaise trail down the front of his ample paunch.

"You Malone?" he said through half-chewed mush. He slapped the burger down on the wrapper spread over his legs and gave Malone a limp, messy handshake.

"I'm the one." Malone said, glancing at the ooze Jensen had smeared on his hand.

Oblivious, Jensen again assaulted his sandwich. "Word has it you're looking for Esther Hunter. You find her yet?"

"No, but I thought you might be able to shed some light on the subject. Do you know her very well? Have you talked to her lately?" Malone discretely smeared the unwanted juices over the back of his jeans.

Jensen masticated for a minute or so, and the turning of cogs was almost audible in the tiny office. "Well, sort of," he said. "I went over to their place once, right after old man Hunter's first heart attack. She had me move some stuff out of their second-floor bedroom into the den on the first."

Suddenly oblivious to Malone's presence, he wolfed the last of the hamburger, and washed the whole mess down with a Coke the size of a half-gallon jug. After slurping and gulping until he sucked air at the bottom, Jensen belched, then snickered like it had been the essence of entertainment.

Malone's vision—about the ranks of classical music aficionados being filled with the suave and sophisticated—had just been severely muddied. "Do you remember anything she said before her husband died? Places they had been, antiques they might have found or purchased?"

Jensen's thick eyebrows sullied about. "Not really. But she cancelled her appearance at a benefit show. Something about finding Mr. Hunter a care facility somewhere in Tarpon Springs close to their house."

He rolled away from the desk, then bent heavily and lifted a beat-up phone book from a stack he used as a footrest. The covers had a history, with names and numbers scribbled at angles. Pieces were torn out and rendered to regions unknown.

"Ah-h. I know it's here somewhere." He squinted at the maze of doodles. "Here it is. Seven Sands Manor. Tarpon Springs."

"I appreciate that," Malone said. "Taking time from your busy schedule."

"No sweat, dude," Jensen said. "Been here so long I do it in my sleep."

I bet you do, Malone thought. "If you hear anything, give me a call," he said, handing him a business card.

His search thus far for the chimerical Mrs. Hunter seemed to be dead-ending at every turn. His feeling was that some unseen hand was steering him away from the exit, in the vein of a lab rat in a maze.

There are in every man the seeds of greatness, the taxi driver told him on the way home. Malone thought it better not to tell the driver that sometimes those seeds fall on infertile ground. He pondered the likes of Barry Jensen and the iceberg receptionist during the silent ride back to St. Pete.

* * *

On Saturday Malone's truck was in the shop and the weather was not cooperating. He made it a day to stay home and catch up on tasks he had put off during the week. Things like eating a decent meal, reading his weekly collections of daily news, cleaning his condo. Simple things, but all were essential to the well-being of body, mind, and soul.

Channel 8's weather radar images showed a cold front moving south toward the Tampa Bay region, due to arrive around eight a.m. Malone knew better than to trust a Florida meteorological forecast, but he took Redford for a walk anyway. The rain arrived at seven, and despite racing back they got drenched in the homestretch.

The outer door buzzer rang through on the house phone as he was pulling off his T-shirt and shorts and hanging them over the shower doors. He took a couple towels to dry Reddy and himself, then grabbed the portable phone and waited for the announcement. A telephone announcement, condo management had said, would spare residents' guests the possible indignity of a wino detailing various bodily functions over a speaker box at the top of his lungs.

Redford wouldn't hold still for drying, so Malone buzzed downstairs. In the background, he heard the rain coming down hard and the speaker was picking up lightning static. He was surprised and delighted to hear Anne Hurt on the other end.

"Anne?" he said. "What are you doing out in this mess?"

Her voice was shivering. "I had to talk to you, Jazz. Can I come up for a while?"

"Of course."

Malone keyed the entry button and heard the lobby door buzz over the phone. She was on the way up...and he was naked.

He quickly pulled on shorts and a robe. Reddy finished drying by himself, leaving dark splotches on the couch and a long, wet streak on the dining room wall. When Anne tapped at the front door, Malone closed Redford off in the study.

She stood in the doorway dressed in white silk blouse and slacks, ankle-strap pumps, and looking like the proverbial wet rag. Wearing a Mayan, patchwork-quilt jacket much like the one Connie had, Anne carried a convoluted umbrella.

"I'm sorry, Jazz," she said, shivering in the air-conditioned hallway.

Malone pulled her inside and she started crying. He showed her to the guest bath and where to find towels. While her clothes were tumbling dry, he prepared coffee for two and crème-filled, Utah scones for three. Redford gobbled his in one bite.

When Anne emerged from the bathroom her hair glowed a palette of wet reflections, and she was wearing the short, green terry-cloth robe Connie had left behind in her angry rush to leave. She sat modestly in a wicker rocker as Malone took a place across from her on the sofa and poured the coffee.

"What's going on?" he said. "You seem upset."

"I don't know what to do about Tony anymore," Anne said.

"What's Tony up to? He working you the way he works?

Anne took a sip of coffee then a bite of the scone before placing it on the dish. Her eyes revealed a floodgate of emotions waiting to be released.

"It's like Tony never has time for me anymore," she said. "Even when he does his mind is always somewhere else. He always seems…angry about something."

It was hard for Malone to fathom where this was leading. He held with the belief that when someone violates that unseen emotional barrier between being friends and sharing intimately deeper thoughts and feelings, ethical distinctions became blurred. Many a friend's relationship had ended bitter and confused for lack of that differentiation.

"Some people have a habit of hurting the ones they love," he professed. "Once the damage is done, they can't or won't take the time to figure out how to make things right. How to return to their intimate state of joie de vivre."

Over the course of a nine-year marriage Malone had been unable to adequately vocalize his feelings for Connie. He had come too late to understand that Connie longed for him to say he loved her, to voice his admiration for her, his affections.

Even now Malone doubted Connie would ever understand that he, like most men, demonstrated love in simple, actionable ways, the embodiment of the writer's undying creed of show versus tell. When the flowers, good music and getaways to intimate places began to fail, their relationship became a mere shadow of its former self, reduced to its essence, bewildered and mute.

"Can you talk to me about it?" Malone went on. "Or is it something you'd rather not discuss?" No longer afraid to delve into mysteries, experience had taught him that life was too short and precious for acting noncommittal with anyone.

"I need to talk about it," she nodded, her eyes wandering over the apartment. She was recognizing, in ways only women seem to understand, the personal touches that bespeak the presence of another woman.

"Last night at Michael's, Tony walked out on me," she said, lingering on the words, watching for his reaction. "I think he's seeing someone else and I don't think he's coming back."

Malone felt he meant nothing to Anne. He was still too confused about his breakup with Connie to get involved with her. "That's not what's bothering you, though," he said. "Is it?"

Anne stood and walked around the coffee table and books separating them, then sat beside him on the sofa, her hands clenched in her lap. When her elbow touched his arm, she turned and gazed wistfully at him.

"I've never known anyone like you, Jazz," she said. "You're handsome, intelligent, relaxed, hiding behind those green eyes all the time. You're like Tony in a lot of ways, but different. You seem to know where you're going in this crazy world. You're nothing like most of the men I've known."

She moved closer and pressed her warmth against him. Her robe had fallen open and her skin was tawny and soft. Malone could feel her heart pulsing strong and inviting.

"You need someone like me, too," she said. "I know about your problems with Connie."

"What do you mean? What's Connie got to do with this?"

Her face wrinkled with concern.

"I thought Tony had called you. He got the divorce papers from Connie's attorney."

Malone stood up, rigid and clenching. His mind writhed like a swarm of poisonous snakes, full of rage and frustration.

"I knew it was coming," he said. "God knows I just wasn't ready for it."

"She doesn't deserve you," Anne said softly, taking his hand and gently pulling him down beside her. "I've searched all my life for someone like you. I've wanted to do this since the day I first saw you with Redford."

She wrapped her arms around him and kissed him, her tongue playing at his lips, her breasts pressing hot indentations into him. His hand found her warm nipple and he slipped willingly over a precipice from which there was no return.

All that had been on hold was in his embrace. In those moments Malone found his rage transformed into desire and his frustrations melting away. Anne unfolded like a rose and drew him in with rhythms as ancient as the seasons.

That night he wrote in his journal while Anne slept. How she could become for him all that a man wants and finds in the arms of a woman. How she would be a balm for his wounds and a kindling for his hopes and desires.

Help him reclaim a sense of innocence along the way.
Artifacts, they were, from another time. Feelings
Malone thought had been lost to the gradual complacency
of age ebbed slowly and sweetly back into his world.

4

Man is born unto trouble, as the sparks fly upward.
Job 5, verse 7

Anne left early the next morning, and Malone drove back to the Hunter place. Suspicions had nagged him throughout the night about something he had seen just before the encounter with Lt. Cobb. Unsure of what that something was, he wanted to take another look inside.

In the dark hours before dawn the birds were beginning to move about and the trees leaned heavily over the yard. Malone backed into the pocket across the two-lane highway where the Plymouth had been parked. Redford trotted at his side up the long, two-track driveway to the house.

Malone jimmied a living room window as open while Redford sat quietly in the deep shadows beneath. He climbed in, and swept the flashlight around the chaotic living room. The carpets emitted a sharp, rancid smell, like Limburger cheese moldering in a cardboard box. An amoeba-like mold had begun crawling one wall toward the ceiling.

The sound of shards of the broken glass that littered the kitchen's checkerboard tiles crunching under his boots reminded him of what he had seen. The cork bulletin board, hanging next to the wall phone.

Malone peeled away the layers and laid them aside until he found a sales invoice for the dagger. Aunty Q had paid a pittance of $75 for the antique knife.

On the back of the receipt a notation referred to a book titled, *Mesoamerican Culture: A Religious Perspective.* The book's price was written beside it. The antique shop where Mrs. Hunter had made her purchase was in the heart of Ybor City. Antigua, C.A. was its name, and one Eduardo Garcia was listed as manager.

The contents of a bookcase had been spilled on the carpet in the living room. Malone found the reference book there, some its pages still soggy from the deluge. A paper clip marked a photo section containing an artist's rendering of the dagger. A newspaper clipping was tucked between the pages.

The article stated that a sacrificial dagger had been discovered in an ancient Mayan compound deep in the jungles of Guatemala. The carved, black-jade dagger had been declared a national treasure by the Guatemalan government. Officials were indicating more of such finds were possible at known but thus far unexplored Mayan compounds.

That made the one existing dagger virtually priceless, Malone thought, explaining Tony Amato's reasons for wanting it retrieved. Was Tony really working with John Tanner and the Guatemalan government to recover the dagger? And if the dagger was that valuable, how did a little shop in Ybor City come to possess it? And who, apparently ignorant of its historical value—not to mention its black-market value—sold it to the shop?

Redford growled outside and let rip with a bark.

Malone ducked as headlights swept across the front windows and lit up the house's interior momentarily.

He clambered out the open window and hit the ground running with Red loping alongside, then hid behind a metal tool shed leaning against the side of the garage. Redford twitched and let out little snorts.

"Quiet, Reddy," he whispered.

A Pinellas County Sheriff's car wheeled up the driveway with its high beams on, and a deputy got out. He clamped a long flashlight under one arm and spoke softly into a small radio attached to his epaulet. He walked quickly around the house, panning his light across the crime-scene tape and onto various windows and doors, then rattling the front and back door locks. Quickly remounting, the deputy disappeared into the black maw of night, streaks of taillights speeding away.

Malone returned to slide the window closed the deputy had missed. He and Redford made like gangbusters getting away. There was no glory in getting caught in flagrante delicto.

Slowed by full-tilt, Monday morning rush hour traffic on I-4 through Tampa, Malone drove east into Ybor City. He was immediately tantalized by the smells of coffee and freshly baked pastries filling the air. Old and wizened Cubans, wearing white shirts with the sleeves rolled-up to their elbows, drank demitasse cups of eyeball-popping espresso at sidewalk cafes. They would gesture emphatically, as, Malone imagined, they discussed Fidel's government and recalcitrant wives.

Two blocks off the main drag a short Latino man was unlocking Antigua, C.A., and setting cheap-looking, yellow and brown Incan knock-off vases to each side of the front door. The last remnants of a light rain trickled down the gutter spouts at the corners of the faded, yellow-brick building as Malone pulled up to the curb. Granite flecks embedded in the octagonal stones of the sidewalk scintillated under an incandescent sun.

"Senior Garcia?" Malone called. "Como esta?"

Eduardo Garcia glanced at him, then turned and went inside.

"So much for Social Skills 101," Malone told Redford, leashing him to the roll bar and pouring water.

Garcia was a short, heavy-set man with a full complement of jet-black hair. His pockmarked face looked garish under the fluorescent shop light hanging low over a crowded display case at one side of the tiny store. With Garcia's eyes following him, Malone wandered the old shop, scanning an odd assortment of antiques and collectibles. Most, he noted, were poor imitations or outright trash. Profitability was not a financial goal here it seemed, or even a serious consideration.

Garcia moved his weight well. Without a sound, he was suddenly standing right next to Malone.

"What you wan'?"

"Just some information, amigo."

"I do beezness, not talk."

Garcia went back and began polishing the top of a small, maple-wood corner table. Tempting fate, he precariously hung one buttock on the back of a beat-up, overstuffed armchair, all the while juggling the small table.

"I gotcha," Malone said, laying a twenty-dollar bill on the display case next to the cinnamon-skinned man. "Will this make it beezness?"

Indifferent, Garcia gave a short, upward head jerk.

"You know anything about an elderly lady by the name of Esther Hunter?" he continued. "Or anything about a dagger she bought here not long ago?"

Garcia's expression went flat. Standing straight up, he grabbed the twenty and flashed a gold-toothed grin.

"I seeck that day," he said. "No here."

"Fine," Malone said. "Maybe you can tell me what became of the dagger. Or were you seeck that day too?"

Garcia glanced towards the rear of the store. He looked at Malone and shook his head.

"I don' know. I box dagger, then ship."

He walked over to the garbage pile of a desk he used and moved stuff around. "Senora Hunter," he read from a notebook, "she has."

"One more question," Malone said, knowing he was chasing his own tail. "Who owns this place?"

Garcia grinned idiotically. "They come, they go, mostly they go. I know only I take money to bank."

"From this place? What money? What bank?"

"We make money," Garcia shrugged. "Banco C.A."

Malone felt doomed and was sure his credit had run out. Garcia laughed nervously and walked away, disappearing into the gloom behind a stained, lace-bordered curtain at the rear. The feeling of being lost in a maze struck him again. One by one, the guideposts were disappearing with regularity.

Francis Bacon once said "there is in human nature generally more of the fool than of the wise." As Malone drove away he wondered, where his conversation with Eduardo Garcia was concerned, which one of them had been more the fool?

* * *

Gladys Thompson was a Pinellas County records clerk. A small, thin-framed, ebony-skinned lady, she wore thick-lens glasses and had a pencil stuck through one of her patterned braids. She was scrolling her computer's video screen through Florida state business licensing records so fast the kaleidoscopic blur was giving Malone a headache.

"There it is."

"How can you read that, Gladys?"

"I did it manually, before a search function ever existed," she said. "It's just habit now."

He peered over her shoulder as she highlighted the

license data on Antigua, C.A. he had asked for.

"That's odd," she said. "The parent company has some kind of special clearance from U.S. Customs called 'Exclusionary.'"

"Special clearance? Doesn't all freight into the U.S. have to go through customs at one point or another?"

"That's what I thought," she said, paging down the record. "But all these guys need is a corporate signature, a custom's inspection stamp, and they're done."

"Somebody must have some heavy notes, way up high in that bureaucratic web called federal government," Malone said.

"Got that right."

How else could unobstructed passage through customs be so seemingly easy to obtain? Or explained?

"Can you print that out for me, please?" Malone said.

Gladys clicked her mouse, and handed over the printed form. "Anything else I can do for you, Jazz?"

"Much appreciated, Ms. Thompson." He laid a small, intricately woven Mayan handbag on the counter. "See if you can find a good home for this."

"Thank-you, Jazz," she smiled. "You didn't have to do that. I'm just doing my job."

"My pleasure, ma'am."

Outside the county building he stood at the counter of a roach wagon sporting a day-glow-orange, striped beach canopy and ice cream decals on every inch of window glass. He read the printout as he sipped at something the vendor called coffee.

Only one thing on the form he didn't already know. The little hole-in-the-wall was owned and operated by a big hole-in-the-wall with the acronym of SWEFAP. No officers listed, no corporate particulars, no management other than Garcia. Nothing.

Malone's picks, it seemed, were leading him further into unknown territory. He sensed a quagmire forming there, pulling him inevitably toward its soft and cloying edges.

* * *

Over the phone, the administrator at Seven Sands Manor in Tarpon Springs said, yes, there was a Mrs. Hunter in residence. When he insisted on the room extension, the woman became pretentious, saying Mrs. Hunter's medications prevented her from holding anything resembling conversation. Malone hung-up, mystified as to the reason Aunty Q had been admitted and who had authorized the placement.

Cautiously driving north on U.S. 19 toward Tarpon Springs, Malone tried hard not to play 'Big Foot' with his four-by-four, and just roll right up over the top of it all. At times like these, he mused on the possibility of someone having had a mean streak when the automobile assembly line came into being.

Full of innocent smiles and enough sweet talk to sicken a con man, Malone finally convinced an emaciated brunette at Seven Sands Manor's nurses' station he was Mrs. Hunter's nephew. Not telling her, of course, everyone within the listening area of WUSF-FM considered themselves Aunty Q's 'relative.'

Escorted to Mrs. Hunter's room, he found her propped up in bed. A tray rested on a bedside table, and she was being spoon-fed a bowl of nasty looking, watery-green vegetable soup.

The male nurse who was sitting on the edge of the bed and feeding her gave Malone a long and lust-filled once-over. He had short, pure white hair, multiple ear-piercings and was clad in a baby-blue smock. He had a heart with an arrow piercing it and dripping blood tattooed on his neck.

"I'm Thomas," he said, half-heartedly dabbing a napkin at Mrs. Hunter's mouth. "Can I help you?"

"Maybe," Malone said. "I need to speak with my aunt."

Once known for her eloquence, Mrs. Hunter looked ghastly. Her white hair was stringy and matted, she was terribly bloated, and had a mottling of large bruises surrounding a needle insertion site on her left arm. An I.V. pump next to the bed clicked as it squirted unknown fluids into her bloodstream. A cast enclosed her right arm and her eyes were glazed.

"I didn't know Esther had any relatives," Thomas said, shoveling gruel faster this time, spilling half down the front of her yellow bib.

"There's probably a lot about Aunty Q you probably don't know," Malone said.

Pulling a chair close to the bed, Malone sat down. Mrs. Hunter gazed at him with vacant eyes. He used her bib to blot rivulets of soup from her mouth and chin.

"For instance?" Thomas said.

"Like who's responsible for her being here?"

Thomas scraped the remains from the bowl and pushed it into her mouth. He yanked the bib from around Mrs. Hunter's neck, then dropped the bowl loudly on the tray and carried it full swish for the door.

"I've got another feeding to do," he said, saying it as if there was a herd of cattle somewhere, anxiously awaiting his caring ministrations.

The man had obviously never heard Aunty Q on Saturday radio. His abrupt exit jettisoned Malone's hope for getting any useful information out of him.

"Tony?" Mrs. Hunter whispered. She was trembling, and her hand shook as she leaned toward the bed's safety rail, trying to touch his face.

"Mrs. Hunter," he said, taking her by the hand. "It's Jasper…Jazz Malone. From church."

She fell back against the pillows, exhausted. Her eyes fluttered closed, then tears trickled down her cheeks.

"Jazz? I thought…" she said, "I thought you were my Tony…where's my Tony?" She coughed and closed her eyes. Turning her head aside, she drifted slowly into what seemed to be a drug-induced stupor.

Malone remembered how Mr. and Mrs. Hunter had gifted so many projects within the church and the community. Money to help build the new Y.W.C.A., furnishings for the cottages and lodge at the Baptist retreat at Moon Lake. Bringing pastries and sandwiches they had prepared themselves every Sunday afternoon to the St. Vincent de Paul's shelter in St. Pete. Paying St. Petersburg Junior College's tuition for nearly a dozen young men and women who would never have had a chance otherwise.

Selfless and loving gestures over a period of a half-century. Who now, he thought, would give the loving care Mrs. Hunter needed in her last years?

Malone gently shook her arm and she opened her eyes slowly. Whatever she was being dosed with, she wasn't going anywhere under her own power. And whoever put her here knew that.

"Can you tell me who did this to you?" he said.

"Who brought you here?"

Mrs. Hunter struggled to form words blurred by drugs. She began crying again.

"That man…hurt me," she whispered thickly. "Wanted my dagger…laughed at me…did this." She tried to lift her broken arm, then let it drop useless in her lap.

"What man did this?" he said, pulling tissue from a box on the bed stand and wiping her nose. Pushing the hair back from her face, Malone was suddenly incensed by obscure forces. Forces that found idle pleasure in brutalizing an elderly woman.

He sat holding her hand. It seemed senior care issues never came under real Congressional scrutiny. Not because eldercare was unregulated, but because many Americans—dispossessed of generational heritages—unwittingly relegated loved ones to such institutions.

They were mausoleums of sorts. Places where mothers and fathers, aunts and uncles, brothers and sisters would in some cases be mistreated and abused. Many often subjected to unsanitary conditions. Confined to haunting prisons of loneliness, where they would simply and eventually die, ignored alike by family and friends.

The Jack Kevorkian's of our world may not be as far off base as we would like to pretend, Malone thought. I could never live this way, if it could be called living.

He didn't want to see Mrs. Hunter suffering. He needed to penetrate her fog, and ask the question for which she might not have an answer.

"Aunty? What was his name? Can you tell me?"

"Those…horrible glasses," she whispered finally, drifting in and out. She raised her head feebly and searched in gray, roiling fogs with dimmed eyes. "James…I think…Gridley."

She slipped away again, into a terrifying darkness where her tormentors came and went at will. But she had found and named her fear for him.

Malone pulled the blanket up around her chin, shielding her from the cold air being ducted relentlessly into the room, then walked out in a blinding rage. Maddened by uncaring, busybody nurses, he stormed past shrunken old men reeking of urine and feces, past old women calling helplessly from beds untended in barren hallways, then crashed recklessly out the front doors.

* * *

Anne was sleeping peacefully when Malone awoke from an odious dream in the small, quiet hours of the morning, sweating and twisted in the sheets. A dream of Machiavellian proportions, where people had been made slaves, pawns in a merciless game of greed and corruption. Their taskmasters were rich men dressed in lab coats or three-piece suits, hiding deep inside decrepit nursing homes filled with moaning and festering bodies.

Standing on the balcony with Redford, Malone listened to the gentle sounds of palm fronds rustling in the breeze. Stars twinkled on the waters of Mirror Lake, their ageless wonders soothing away the hopeless, empty feelings he had dragged from a restless sleep.

Somewhere in this city roamed a man whose soul was possessed by demons, whose actions were dictated by greed and whose reality was predicated by his own betrayal of all that was just. Malone knew he would find this evil man and teach him the pain of Mrs. Hunter, of all the Mrs. Hunters. This man would soon learn of his own personal hell right here on earth.

While Redford ground the remains of a rawhide chew bone to a stub with his scissor-like teeth, Malone sat at his desk close by the light of his stationmaster's lamp at five a.m., trying to piece together what little he had gathered on the case. Few details about—or reasons for—Mrs. Hunter's confinement were evident. And he knew nothing of the dagger's location.

The only real clue thus far involved a man possibly named James Gridley. He didn't know where to begin looking for this man. Who had hired him and his knack for menacing? There were other vague connections, Malone felt, waiting behind corners it seemed, to leap at him and gorge on his sanity.

Intending to leave a message, he called the offices of Baxter, Brannon, Moss and Amato. He was surprised to hear Tony's voice on the other end.

"You burning the midnight oil?" Malone said. "Or pushing an early start?"

"I don't have time to talk," Tony said. "I've got an eight o'clock filing deadline and I still have motions to rewrite."

"I located Mrs. Hunter," Malone said.

Tony stopped breathing, then punched a number on another phone in the background. "I'll call you back in a few minutes," he said, then disconnected.

"What is it you need, Jazz?" Tony said, his voice filled with suspicion when Malone's phone rang a few minutes later.

"To settle my expense account," Malone said.

"You find the dagger?"

"Not yet, but I fulfilled one part of our contract, and I'd like to get paid for it."

Tony rustled some papers and then was silent.

"I'll pay you the second thousand," he said, "but our accountant will have to look over the why's and when's of your expenses to date."

Instincts told him Tony was stalling; four previous jobs and he had never hesitated on paying fees. This time it was almost as if Tony knew something, something that was a great force weighing and wearing him down, pitting him against himself.

"Drop it in the mail, Tony," Malone said. "I don't have time to pick it up."

When the newspaper dropped by the door,
Malone lay on the couch and scanned the Monday edition
of the St. Petersburg Times. Buried on page 8A was an
article dealing with the Rosetta stone of the Guatemalan
Mayans. It related how videotape, showing several
different views of a 4 by 5 foot, milky-covered limestone
slab, was circulating among art dealers and
archaeologists. The Cancun slab was covered with
hieroglyphics dating back 1,500 years. Tomb robbers
were offering the slab on the black market for $75,000—
a chunk.

Actually priceless, the article went on to say, the
slab was one of thousands of artifacts looted from ancient
burial sites in Mexico and Guatemala. Artifacts with
untold historical value, smuggled illicitly every year into
the U.S. for the sake of avarice. With their attention
focused on the illegal drug trade, U.S. Customs officials
could do little to stem the tide of stolen artifacts.

A fitful, orange sun hung low among somber clouds
over Tampa Bay when he left Anne a note asking her to
call later. Taking Redford for his morning ritual in the
salt-laden airs along the winding sidewalks of North
Shore beach, Malone stopped at a coffee stand for a cup

of cappuccino.

Redford lifted his leg on a bush near the Vinoy Yacht Basin, with its pickup-stick array of swaying mastheads and melodically clinking riggings. On a nearby corner, a bag lady dressed in a ragged, brown overcoat and a dirty pair of tennis shoes fed a loaf of moldy bread to a madcap flock of seagulls. Her shopping cart was loaded with plastic bags filled with magazines, newspapers and bottles, a variety of societal detritus.

It was a poignant reminder of Mrs. Hunter's predicament. Malone rang Lt. Cobb's office and left his cell phone number with the dispatch officer. When he called back, Cobb's voice sounded hollow, like he hadn't slept well.

"What is it this time, Malone?"

"You might like to know," he said. "I found Mrs. Hunter."

"Oh, yeah?" Cobb said. "Any explanation worth hearing?"

"She had a broken arm. Somebody had her confined to a Tarpon Springs nursing home. They're flooding her bloodstream with sedatives and God knows what else."

Redford pulled at his leash and the bag lady and her attending flock had drifted further down the beach walk. Malone was out of coffee.

"Shit happens," Cobb said. "Wouldn't be the first old lady to fall down and do some damage."

"It damn sure wasn't her rocking chair gone haywire, Vern. She was assaulted. Something's going on, and I'd like to find out exactly what it is and who's behind it."

Back at the refreshment stand, Malone had the attendant refill his cup before unclipping Reddy and letting him run, following him down to waters' edge. The waves were clear and sparkling in the early light, breaking in foaming curls on the shoreline. Fiddler crabs scurried back to their holes as Reddy barked and chased after them.

"She give you a name?" Cobb asked. "Might simplify matters a little."

"James Gridley," Malone said. "From what I could gather, might be the same screwball who took out my truck's main glass."

"Gridley, Gridley..." Lt. Cobb muttered, rummaging papers in the background. "Sounds familiar... Okay... Gridley James is the perp's name, not James Gridley. An ex-con, been walking in dip all his life."

"It appears he's about to step in it again."

"Right. You and Mrs. Hunter come down and swear out complaints. Who knows? Maybe this toad will pop up again."

"See you in about an hour," Malone said. "I don't think Mrs. Hunter is going to make it, though with her liquid diet and extended sleep cycle."

"You'll figure something out," Cobb said, then hung up.

* * *

Sitting in his office with his boots propped on the open bottom drawer of his desk, Lt. Cobb was puffing on what looked to be a fifty-cent cigar. His tie was tucked into his shirt, military style, and his sleeves were rolled up. He was grinning ear to ear.

"What do you say, cowboy?" he said. "Run into any brick-flopping birds lately?"

"Looks like I might have jump-started your day. Glad to have been of assistance."

Sitting on one of the padded, gray metal chairs, Malone placed a Styrofoam cup of burnt coffee on the corner of Lt. Cobb's desk, hoping it would go away.

"Yes sir," Cobb said. "Got something to work with now."

"Gridley James."

"Right."

Dropping the cigar in the ashtray, Cobb wheeled his chair backwards around the desk to a computer that stood to one side of a portable strategy board. He pecked at the keyboard with two fingers, grubbing about dumb machines under his breath.

"Hot damn, I did it," he said, looking in amazement at the computer screen. "Is this your brick shitter?"

The computer image of Gridley James gave him the grainy look of an unshaven drunk just off a three-day binge, foul-tempered and ugly. Malone shook his head in disgust.

"With longer hair and mirrored glasses, yeah, that's him."

Cobb looked doubtful. "You sure? There's a lot of mean mothers out there look just like him."

"I'd recognize that beak anywhere."

James's nose resembled a comma. Bent to one side, it looked as if it had been mashed onto his face as an afterthought by some jesting, retsina-infused god.

Lt. Cobb wheeled back to his desk and picked up his phone. "All right, bud, I'll get the avalanche sliding." He made two quick calls, then propped his feet up and stuck the dead cigar back in his mouth. "Just sign the complaint on the way out. We'll do the rest."

Malone stood by the computer screen reading the rap sheet on Gridley "Ax" James. Two back-to-back runs in the Florida penitentiary. Five years on numerous aggravated assault charges, a six-year stint for armed robbery. The kind of man who likely thought it entertaining to brutalize old people. An animal that needed to be put away permanently—if they could find him.

"What's on your mind, honch?" Cobb said.

Malone sat down again, trying to put a face with the telephone voice he had heard at the Hunter place. A voice having the ring of self-assurance couched in soft-spoken words. Someone who might know when and where to find Gridley James.

"I need some information." he said, taking a sip of the charred coffee.

Cobb's face hardened as he relit his cigar. "The only thing you're going to get from me is advice," he said, kicking his boots up on top of his desk and blowing a cloud of smoke. "Stay the hell out of this mess."

"I'm already involved. I just want a little skinny on a guy named John Tanner."

Lt. Cobb dropped his feet to the floor and leaned forward, glaring, as if someone had just pissed in the punch bowl.

"How you figure John Tanner into this?" he said. "Man's an upright citizen. On the sheriff's advisory board for what, eight, ten years? Been a banker for God knows how long."

Malone knew he had to tread softly. He didn't want to step on any upright citizen's toes, much less leave Cobb feeling like his Mr. Clean might be involved in questionable dealings.

"At Tanner's request, Tony hired me to find Mrs. Hunter."

"And? You found her, got paid, *finis*!"

"Yeah, sure. Finis." Picking up his coffee, Malone walked to the door. "If you see James, tell him I mean to collect on my windshield."

After signing the complaint form, Malone stood in the main lobby reading the wanted posters. Cobb was right about one thing. These guys did look alike. The spawn of old Diablo himself.

The lieutenant was very wrong about something else though. Malone was not finis.

7

The first time Malone had dined with Connie at Michael's, on Beach-side Drive, it was a languid night in June and the restaurant had been nearly empty. A simple decor, the eatery had round tables covered in white linen, each warmly lit with red candles stuck in French-label wine bottles. Porcelain miniatures and under-spoken paintings gave it the subdued aura of an intimate, Parisian enclave. Waiters dressed in crisply starched, black and white uniforms served with quick but polite efficiency. The food and wine were complimented by the softly chorded phrasings of a jazz guitarist playing nearby.

This night, dinner with Anne and a concert afterward, was to be one of magic and charm. In a rush, Malone had left his truck standing with two wheels riding the curb. Anne's Porsche was cooling neatly in front of Michael's when he arrived. Car parks stood nearby casting envious glances at the green sports car.

Anne was sitting backwards at a small piano bar in the back of the dimly lit room. She was leaning against the bar and sipping a glass of wine and laughing at something a man wearing a tuxedo and sitting close was saying over the low noise of the crowded restaurant. Dressed in a shimmering, sea-green silk evening gown with lace sleeves and pearl button clasps open down the front, she revealed a vee of tanned skin to below her navel.

Her hair was swept back on one side, revealing a delicate and supple neck. She laughed, then put her hand on his cheek, familiar and warm. He leaned closer and kissed her.

Discouraged, Malone turned to leave but Anne saw him and waved for him to come over. She retrieved her clutch and wineglass from the bar as he waded toward her between busy tables and rushing waiters.

The man moved to another place in the crowded room and immediately engaged another woman in conversation. Malone realized it was Tony, looking much different under the subdued lighting.

Anne's eyes sparkled in the candlelight and she pulled Malone's face down to hers and kissed him. "God, I love you!" she said, "and I'm famished. Let's eat and then go listen to some wonderful orchestra music."

Tony stood at the bar drinking from a tumbler and peering in their direction. He swirled his drink, then turned away and gestured impatiently at the bartender.

Malone ordered surf and turf, and ten minutes later it was served on a sizzling platter. It smelled delicious, but the more he thought about Tony hitting on Anne, the less appetite he had.

"What was that all about?" he said. His taste for the food and Michael's had evaporated. "You and Tony. At the bar."

"Oh, you know Tony," Anne said. "He thinks every woman he takes to bed worships at his feet." She took another bite, then laid her fork down when she realized Malone was staring at her.

"What's wrong, Jazz? It's not like you to sulk this

way."

"I just thought it was all over between you two," he said. "The way he was hanging on you, it looked like…."

"I don't believe it!" she laughed. "You're jealous!" She got up and took his hand, pulling him from his seat. "Come on, let's get out of here. We'll take my car."

Anne opened the T-tops on the Porsche and then wheeled through downtown traffic and onto I-275. Speeding through the hot, night air with her hair trailing in the wind, the music of Ravel charged her soul.

"What about the concert?" Malone said. He had loved classical music since he was a boy hearing bumblebees and cannon shots from another century for the first time.

"We'll go some other time," she said. "Did I ever take you to the lake?"

She smiled devilishly. Slipping her hand up his leg, Anne's fingers traced lines across his zipper then down between his thighs to linger and tease.

"Can't say that you have," he said. "How did you happen to find it?"

Bothered by the sudden change in plans, he didn't really want to know. Her hand was bringing him to a pulsing hardness and he found what little resistance he had failing.

Anne turned off the interstate, sped past St. Petersburg-Clearwater Airport, then headed down a long, dark stretch of two-lane road toward Cove Cay. The car's headlights painted the deep descent into the woods with sweeping cones of light.

"My father owns about sixty acres out here," she said, turning onto a two-track road that wound further back into the utter blackness. "Tony brought me out to look at a cabin he had had built for me on the lake. That was long before we broke up. I haven't been out here since."

She stopped at the end of a narrow dirt road. The headlights panned out over the murky depths of a lake with a small, variegated-sand beach surrounding its edges. The palmettos had been cut back about twenty feet around the lake and up to the cabin. Along the new perimeter, hurricane fencing had been erected, with the posts and lower edges of the chain link anchored in concrete.

Malone guessed it had been fenced to keep out alligators. In this area, some of them were large enough to swallow a calf whole.

Anne switched off the engine and opened her door, then kicked off her heels and ran down to the gate and swung it open. Giggling like a truant teenager, she unbuttoned her dress in the Porsche's headlights and dropped it in the sand at water's edge. Then, sans clothing, dove headlong into the lake.

"Come on in," she yelled when she surfaced, "it's warm!" She swam back toward the shoreline and stood half-immersed, looking at Malone shyly. Her breasts glistened in the beams of the Porsche's headlights.

"I will," he said, laying his coat and tie on the hood and unbuttoning his shirt. "But I've got this growing problem."

Anne waded out and kneeled in front of him, her hands pulling at his belt and unzipping his pants. Sliding his briefs down, she engulfed him with her mouth, drawing him to full attention.

"Does that help?" She stood and kissed him, then walked back to the water. Her hips swayed sensuously.

Swimming in the dark waters, their hands played at each other's body, mouths hot against each other's lips and then submerged, at each other's sex. When the moon wandered from behind the clouds Malone turned off the car lights, then lay on a blanket Anne had brought from the cabin and spread at lakeside and made love with her.

On top of him, her legs grasped his hips and she slowly rode him. Her body arced against his in the canopy of moonlight, her urgent sighs becoming wild cries across the night. When their ecstasy flowed as one, they soared together with racing hearts among molten clouds and diamond-studded, velvet skies.

8

On his first day of fourth grade, Malone's teacher, a full-blooded Seminole, came to school dressed in her native garb. She wore a lace-fringed blouse that had long sleeves and rounded neckline and wildflowers were embroidered across the chest and a billowing skirt, seeming to have every color of the rainbow woven into it.

It rustled with delicate sound of crinolines as she walked. Her delicately woven bracelets, the cloth inlaid with strings of wood beads and tiny shells, tocked softly as she proudly related her ancestors' history to his class. He became forever enamored that day, with all things fashioned by hand.

Many years later, during an unplanned trip to the remote villages of Guatemala, Malone rediscovered his fascination with native handicrafts in the works of the Mayans. Beautifully woven clothing, colorful bags and patterned blankets, bridal-veil fringed hammocks and silver jewelry that displayed hours of pains-taking labor. All became a part of his enduring passions.

To satisfy his heart's desires he began importing Mayan goods, at first bringing back small amounts. When the demand outpaced his meager supplies, he hired a freight-forwarding company and resigned himself to the labyrinth of frustrations known as U.S. Customs. The lessons he learned then became his armor for the awaiting ordeal, when he paid a visit to the Port of Tampa U.S. Customs office in search of the phantasmagoria known as SWEFAP.

At channel's end, sitting in a long row of tall, sheet-metal quayside warehouses, the building's modern construction looked out of place. A white stucco, up-ended cracker box warehouse, it had a flexible garage door rising fifteen feet up one side of the building. Small meshed windows on the first floor were shaded by vertical blinds, and the large, mirrored doors at the front were blinding in the afternoon sun.

The mercury was pushing ninety and the harbor was at low tide. A panoply of unsavory odors wafted a across the docks. Pier-pilings reeked of tar pitch and diesel oil, and the saltwater mudflats were littered with putrescent seaweed. A requisite, desiccating fish added its malodorous bloom to the sweltering cast.

Malone parked and poured Reddy a big bowl of water from a gallon jug, then tied him to a rain tree standing with its oblong, dark foliage hanging over a scarred wooden bench facing out over the glassy surface of the channel.

"No seagull munching!" he threatened, heading for the customs house and shaking a finger. "I'm watching you."

Redford gulped the water with his whole snout pushed into the bowl. He let out a juicy burp, did the eggbeater with his tail stub, then sat under the tree with his tongue lolling out.

Cold air washed over Malone when he opened the Customs office door. The agent on duty was wearing dark blue pants and a light blue shirt with a small I.D. badge that read, 'W. Allen,' clipped to the collar. He had his elbows leaning on the counter and was paging through a sports equipment catalog. Quietly closing the book, he slipped it under the counter and stood with arms crossed and an irritated look on his face.

"We're about ready to lock-up for the day," W. Allen smirked.

"Three p.m.?" Malone said. "Packing it in already?"

"Just admin," he said. "Remote stations take over at night."

"I'm looking for some information," Malone said, "on a company that receives its materiel through the Port."

W. Allen looked as if he had just had bubonic plague breathed on him. Glancing at his watch he sighed.

"Can't be much help this late in the day," he said. "An active receiver takes at least three days to get a full report."

Standard procedure, Malone thought, hurry up and wait.

Expensive, taxpayer subsidized computers meant nothing. Routine foot dragging by the federal government was still, as his fellow swabbies used to say, 'same-old, same-old.'

"The company is called SWEFAP," Malone said. "There a registry I could look at? Something with the company names and listings?"

"You feeling lucky?" W. Allen said, grinning as he bent below the counter. He dropped a hardback, ring binder of computer printout sheets eight inches thick on the counter top and turned it around. "You might find it in this—if you're quick."

Malone looked through the listings. The bad news

was, instead of alphabetical ordering, the companies were arranged numerically by U.S. Custom's account numbers. The good news was, the companies' board members were listed with the freight data.

"You got one hour," W. Allen said, looking at his watch again. He turned and walked into a supervisor's windowed office and spoke in a low voice to a thickly muscled man with a handlebar mustache. Stone-faced, the man eyeballed Malone from behind his desk and nodded at something had W. Allen said. He dialed a telephone number, spoke a few words and hung-up, then he and W. Allen shot barbed looks at Malone.

Malone quickly scanned the pages, looking for company names beginning with Southern or Southwest Florida. What he found were dozens of pages, hundreds of business names beginning the same way, all in small type.

After forty-five minutes of straining his eyes were watering, but he finally found it: Southwestern Florida Agro Products, the only SWEFAP listed. Malone jotted down names and closed the book, then signaled the agent he was done.

The deadbolt slammed home after Malone closed the door, then all the blinds on the windows were quickly closed. Not yet four p.m., and he felt like he had just gotten the bum's rush.

Most of the longshoremen in this section of the port it seemed had cleared out and gone home. A few straggler freight clerks were sliding the big doors of warehouses closed and locking them. Some of them were heading, Malone imagined, for the bare apartment, the TV dinner and a six-pack, before falling asleep in front of the idiot box.

Shadows were long and canted as he walked to his truck, trying to fit the turns of the maze together. He had a good feeling about his discovery, but it still wasn't clear where the one piece he had found fit the bigger picture.

A big engine gunned a couple piers over, its pulleys squealing under the load as it winched cargo onto a dock. The sounds echoed off the warehouses.

The powerful engine and squealing sounds got closer, and a moment later, Malone realized they weren't from a cargo winch. A black Cadillac with smoke pouring from its rear tires fishtailed around the corner then raced straight at him.

9

In a dead run, Malone wove back and forth across the alley, looking for something solid to hide behind. The Caddy screamed toward him and he jumped up on an old winch-tower lying alongside a warehouse.

The Caddy slammed into the winch's framework and bounced Malone up onto the windshield. He grabbed the windshield wiper and held on as the driver jacked it in reverse and burned the tires backing down the alley. The driver braked hard, shifted into drive, and floored it. Swerving from one side to the other, he braked again and slid to a stop, the engine roar dying away to a hot idle.

Malone landed on the pavement and lay in shock. His ears were ringing and his nose was bleeding; more blood trickled off his fingers.

Reddy bucked hard at his leash and had his teeth bared. He was growling savagely and barking, trying to break free of the tree.

The Caddy's door swung open and Gridley James got out. He was tall and wiry, wore a sweatshirt with no sleeves, and had tattoos covering both arms and his neck. A stained sweatband hung low over his forehead, nearly touching mirrored sunglasses.

"Dumb fuck," he said in a nasally drawl. "You ain't got the message?" He walked up next to Malone and squatted down. "Next time you come nosing around somebody else's bidness, you ain't gonna be so lucky as you was this time."

As James got back in the car, Malone sat up. James grinned and gunned the engine, put the car in drive, locked-up the front brakes and buried the accelerator. The rear tires broke loose, whizzing at high speed, and smoke billowed out in putrid clouds. Malone quickly rolled to one side as the Caddy went screaming past and around the corner out of sight.

Malone sat with Redford in the truck, shaking like a leaf as he stanched the flow of blood from his nose. James's second assault had reconnected him to a deep-seated fear lying burrowed within for more than twenty years. It was a vague fear, haunting him on the back streets of Honolulu, the fear of an unseen evil, waiting in dark corners to wreak havoc on his body and mind.

The evil that Gridley James represented was tangible and potent. Malone's dread then and now lay in not knowing when or where they would strike. Of not knowing when they would visit death upon him, slipping in and out of his life in the dead of night. Waiting for the perfect, silent moment to cripple him or even kill him.

Both SWEFAP and Antigua, C.A. had John Tanner's mark on them. More than just a banker, it appeared that at least one of the upright citizen's ventures might have stolen artifacts written all over it. Understanding was slow in coming, but Gridley James was not the evil Malone knew he should fear.

10

The silent urgency of other people's lives bidding for a piece of Malone's time pulsed its red beacon from the answering machine in the dark apartment. He turned on lights, opened a can of food for Redford and a beer for himself, hit replay on the machine, then sat reading his mail and listening to messages.

The first message was from a Tex-Mex vendor, asking about more Mayan blankets. The second; one of his short stories had caught the attention of a literary agent who wanted to see more. Then there was Anne, wanting him to come to dinner at her place around nine that evening.

The last message, only three words, was both surprising and intriguing.

"Don't get involved," it warned, in a soft, even voice.

The Snell Isle neighborhood was home to many of St. Petersburg's old-money families and influential politicos, with large, stately mansions and sweeping lawns dotted with towering palms and wrought iron yard ornaments. Had Anne not told him her apartment was behind the biggest house on the block, Malone would have gotten lost.

The winding streets and boulevards of the ritzy island began at the bridge spanning Coffee Pot Bayou. Curving around the edges of Tampa Bay, they threaded through the class-conscious neighborhood like giant pretzels.

Malone pulled into an alleyway behind Anne's apartment and parked. She was standing on the upstairs balcony smiling and waving.

"Come around the side," she called. "Through the gate."

After negotiating a massive iron gate, Malone climbed the stairs two at a time and stopped at the top railing. The mansion's football-length rear lawns swept around an Olympic-sized swimming pool, then up a slope to the main house.

Wrapped in birdcage screening, the pool was lit with flood lamps above and below, its waters shimmering and clear in the warm night air. The entire compound was bordered with goldenrod red cannas lilies, and pompous grass. Towering thick hedges of Ligustrum, trimmed and squared, shielded the perimeter.

Anne slipped her arm around his waist and squeezed. She was wearing the green silk and lace outfit she had worn at Michael's. Her hair flowed around her shoulders and an alluring fragrance lingered all around her. She looked ravishing.

"Impressive, isn't it?" she said. "It's my parent's place, but they're adamant about their privacy, even with me. I was lucky to get this apartment."

"What does a man do for a living to be able to afford a place like this?" Malone said. "He's got to have a bankroll the size of Fort Knox or a relative named Rockefeller."

Anne laughed and said, "No Rockefellers in our family tree that I'm aware of, but he has done well with his investments. You'd never know it though. He comes home from work, shuts off all the phones, then he and mom sit in front of the television, eating dinner and channel surfing."

She kissed him again, then took his hand and pulled him inside her apartment. "Will you pour the champagne," she said, "while I put dinner on the table?"

A bottle of Dom Perignon nested in a sterling-silver bucket of ice. Nearby, two rose-petal flutes waited on a side table.

Malone poured the champagne as Anne disappeared into the kitchen. With glass in hand, he stood in the middle of the living room and took in her domain.

The apartment was huge, with an open-air floor plan. Clusters of white, Italian-leather couches curved around the walls. Hindu statuettes stood frozen in dance. Jade elephants of every size, shape and setting were scattered about the room.

All pointed in the same direction, Malone mused.

An eclectic mixture of modern art interposed with Native American shields and headdresses hung on the walls. Muted-light photos and portraits of Anne from nascence to present, reflecting some of her life's intimate moments.

A bamboo divider stood between the living and dining areas, where an upright glass case displayed her collection of weapons: sabers, jewel-handled stilettos, samurai swords, and razor-thin scalpels. The varieties seemed endless. And, undeniably dangerous.

"Are you hungry?" Anne said, watching him and sipping champagne. "I hope so. I made Beef Tartar, with pearl onion au jus and white potatoes."

"The way to a man's heart," Malone said, "bloody champagne and aged steak—or is it the other way around?"

She laughed, then walked around the apartment lighting candles and incense and turning out lights. In the dining area she lit two long-stem, white candles in ornately carved holders standing in the center of the table beside a pair of crystal swans with their necks intertwined. She put Chopin on the CD player, then dimmed the chandelier over the table.

A truly sensory experience, they ate slowly. The only sounds were the soft rustlings of silk curtains and the mesmerizing strains of piano nocturnes. Anne was quite lovely, her eyes reflecting the flickering glow of candlelight, her lips moist with champagne.

"Would you like dessert?" she asked, laying her fork across her plate.

"I don't know," Malone said. "I'm not sure I could eat another bite."

"It's fresh strawberries and French chocolate sauce," she said. "But you don't have to eat it right now."

She had slipped off her heels and was wiggling her stocking toes between his legs. She had a seductive look in her eyes, and unbuttoned her dress.

"We could wait, and eat it in bed…after."

"I love the way you think," Malone said. "You're the only woman I know who has the presence of mind to serve dessert before she serves dessert."

"And I love your body. As for your mind, well…." Anne shed her dress as she ran giggling toward the bedroom.

Malone sat at the table absorbing the spirit of her

home, finishing his champagne and wishing it could last forever but knowing it wouldn't. At times, the only way he could get by was to will the world out of existence, only to have it crash back in unexpectedly.

"It's awfully quiet in here," he said, nudging the bedroom door open and carrying in champagne refills. When his eyes adjusted in the dim light, he nearly dropped the glasses.

Anne had extinguished all but one candle, lit a stick of incense, and was reclining on black silk sheets. Beautifully bare, her hair was splayed in silken, blush-blonde strands across the pillow. With one hand at her nipples and the other between her legs, she was playing a nocturne of her own making.

When she arched her back and slid moaning over the edge, Malone's remaining hope evaporated. He shed several buttons as he stripped off his shirt, then hopped to the bed with his pants around his ankles. When he finally entered her, she came again, biting his shoulder and pulling his hands to her breasts, whispering, "I love you, Jazz…I love you," over and over.

She wrapped her legs around his back and let him plunge to her clinging depths, carrying him with words she shared wetly in his ear up to a hot, electric citadel. A place where their bodies melded into one and their earthly bonds dropped aside like the petals of a rose, to drift softly away on currents of eventide.

11

$\mathbf{M}$alone had fallen asleep in the cool air of the bedroom, satisfyingly exhausted and still tender from his ordeal at the docks, when he was awoken by a sharp sound. He slipped back down, thinking it a dream, then heard it again. What seemed, far away in his half-awake state, like a metallic click.

Anne was lying asleep on her side, her arm draped over his chest. He gently pulled away and slipped on his briefs, then padded groggily out to the kitchen, looking for something to eat and the source of the strange sound.

Malone turned on the light and squinted against the glare. And got sucker-punched....

When he was on active duty in Hawaii, Malone's communications division had "volunteered" him to box in a smoker exhibition. A gig where amateurs pound each other for three, three-minute rounds. He went three minutes with a man a foot shorter and thirty pounds lighter than him, before the guy launched a right hook that connected with his jaw. Malone went down under the lights, hitting the mat like a ton of bricks.

Before the referee waved the smelling salts under his nose, Malone remembered feeling as though he were at the bottom of a well, lying in a pool of molasses a foot thick. He could hear everything being said but didn't understand a word of it, and was unable to move a muscle.

…That's where he lay in Anne's kitchen: at the bottom of the well, being sucked down by molasses and the timekeeper's bell ringing in his ears. Whoever had plowed him had disappeared, and Malone's arms and legs felt like they were glued to the floor.

Anne's screams jolted him out of the haze like a quick shot of the salts, and he struggled to get up. He stumbled down the hallway, crashing against walls and bumping shelves and tables before collapsing on the bedroom floor.

Gridley James had his shiny magnum tucked in his belt, and was leaning over the bed, yanking Anne by her hair. The raw smell of whiskey and stale sweat pervaded the air.

"Thievin' bitch! How you like this?" James said, ugly and laughing, slapping her face and breasts.

"I didn't steal it!" she screamed, shielding her head and crying as his blows rained down on her. She tried to get away, but James knocked her back on the bed, then leaned over and grabbed her again.

"Whoa, whore, I ain't done playin' yet!" he said, yanking her hair viciously. "You gonna tell me where it is or I'm gonna cut it outta ya!"

"I don't have it," she whimpered.

Malone shook his head, trying to wake-up from this horrible nightmare. He struggled to his feet and grabbed James' raised arm, wanting to kill him.

"Hey, peckerhead wants to play too!"

James let go of Anne and swung a roundhouse that ricocheted off Malone's head and sent him reeling backwards. Then he was on him, punching his face, pummeling him to the floor. As Malone slid away into blackness he heard Anne screaming, pleading for James to stop.

Malone floated numbly in a dark world of colluding images. A world where thick, bloated birds hunched fetidly over the carrion of his body and brain, eating away at viscous memories. Of being beat, then of Anne being beat and raped on the floor beside him. Her quiet sobbing.

Another voice came later, deep from within the well. Distorted, strange, intangibly familiar.

* * *

Malone clawed his way out of a pool of blackness. His head and face throbbed, his whole body ached and his eyelids were glued together. The pain in his arm was excruciating. Slowly he opened his eyes and stared, trying to focus, then realized there were sprays of blood on the ceiling and walls. And he was covered in blood.

Sharp pains shot through his ribs and left arm as he stood, and he was horrified by what lie before him. Blood, freckled and splotched on a chair. A large, coagulated pool on the bed. Splashes on the mirror and dresser.

James had called Anne a thieving bitch, and she had denied. He had said he would cut it out of her and still she denied.

Malone reeled through the living room, then to the kitchen. Every light in the apartment was blazing, and Gridley James was gone.

Anne was nowhere to be found.

12

All living beings it is said whether king or pauper, genius or imbecile, human or animal, reach a crisis in their lives when every conceivable pattern of thought dissolves, and the primal instinct for survival takes over. Simply stated, the body chooses fight or flight.

Hours later Malone found himself driving down the sandy, two-track road leading to the lake at Cove Cay. His imagination played tricks on him, putting ghostly, human forms in his path that disappeared into the dark underbrush. His arm hung limp and painful at his side and his head and ribs ached terribly.

Sunrise glowed at the edge of the world and the thunderheads of a summer storm towered over the Gulf. Lightning danced between the clouds and the thunder rumbled. It would be a heavy rain when it came. In the distance sirens wailed, getting closer by the moment.

His headlights illuminated the still darkened road and taillight reflections winked back at him from the end of the path by the lake. Killing the engine, Malone rolled up behind the car and doused the lights. It was a Mercedes, parked deep within a wall of blackness.

Tony walked out from the shadows carrying a pint bottle of Jack Daniels. He took the last swig, then lobbed the bottle into the underbrush.

"Knowing Annie the way I do," he slurred, leaning on the window ledge of Malone's truck. "She probably brought you here not long ago. And knowing you the way I do, I figured you'd probably come back here. I called the cops."

Tony said it jokingly, like he was making up some half-baked scheme the way he used to in college. But the sirens had gotten much closer, and red and blue lights were strobing from the direction of the highway.

"How did you find out?" Malone said, his thoughts a panicky blur of nightmarish images.

"You forget 'bout Annie and me?" Tony said. "I got a key. I saw the whole bloody mess. I didn't know you were capable of anything like that."

That interminable whisper again, telling him there was something else. Malone pushed the door open, forcing Tony to move back, then stepped out. This was beyond reasonable.

"Take a look at me, Tony," he said, clenching his teeth, getting in Tony's face. "Look at my arm. You think I'm capable of doing this to myself?" Malone tried to raise his arm, but the pain was overwhelming and shock was setting in.

Shaken, Tony stepped back and gazed at Malone's bruised face and blood-soaked clothes, then turned as if to run, looking at his hands then staring at Malone. Deep in Tony's eyes Malone saw the animal he had become in the fleeing, and that somehow, he suspected his pal was in the staying.

Two Pinellas County Sheriff's cars wheeled up and slid to a stop, then two more slid in beside them. Deputies jumped out and stood behind their doors, guns drawn and pointed, shouting, "get down on the ground."

would tell them to bang a copper slave with the M-27 mustsight. It made a jillions problems, progressively tens. He had a gun in his. He reached for a handy, then said, "The Taroon happen "Sacred." "It out how you fingerprints and boves on....

He bent pulsating peasled. They're at it, apparently, we speak," she said. "They like your plan oil over the place.

They had read his rights, slapped the bracelets on him and stuck Malone in the back of a patrol car by the time Lt. Cobb showed up. The officer who locked the cuffs had put an extra squeeze on them when he heard Malone's arm was injured. He said it wouldn't be good if Malone moved it around too much.

Cobb went straight to where Tony leaned against his Mercedes, talked with him for several minutes, then came over to the squad car. Tired and angry, he rubbed his face with both hands, then opened the door.

"I don't know what the hell I'm going to do with you, Malone," he said. "You got yourself so far down in the hole on this one...." He bit the end off a cigar and stuck it in his mouth. He studied Malone, chewing at the cigar's end, then rolled it back and forth between his lips.

"Don't know if there's anything I can do," he went on, shaking his head and sighing.

"I didn't do anything, Vern," Malone said. "You could take these cuffs off me; I'm not going anywhere."

Cobb squinted at him. "Well, somebody did something. You're the only one soaked in blood, and it sure didn't come from a couple of shaving cuts."

He released the handcuffs, then took out a cell phone and punched in a number. Malone rubbed his bad arm, trying to ignore the pains knifing through it.

"Yeah, Sissy?" he said, "Lt. Cobb. Send me a lab

crew, and tell them to bring a couple divers with them. What? That's right, Tanner's property...no, no, in Cove Cay. Richards is out front." He paused for a minute, then said, "Oh, I almost forgot. Send an EMT out here too. Our boy's got a broken arm."

He hung up looking puzzled. "They're at the apartment as we speak," he said. "They found your prints all over the place."

Malone caught bits and pieces of what Cobb was saying, but couldn't get out of his mind what he had said before, about this being Tanner's property.

"Vern," he said. "Who owns the apartment?"

"The other end of this noose you're hanging from?" he said. "That's sitting on the back of John Tanner's primary residence."

Tony drove up alongside the squad car and powered the window down. His face was a blank slate. "I'll call an attorney," he said to Malone. "I'll have someone meet you at the county jail."

As Tony drove away, Malone felt his cards begin to fall. He was tired and disappointed, bitter enough now to let them fall where they may. He was no longer afraid of Gridley James and his bag of tricks. James had beaten what fear there was out of him, but had left him bleeding and alive.

He remembered the telephone call and a voice warning him away. It was John Tanner's daughter Malone loved, and it was Tanner's unseen face he feared most. Tanner had inflicted damage for the breech of his domain. The web he had spun left Malone with no avenue of escape, no way to stop the banker from destroying his world.

14

When he first arrived, Malone was assigned to the prison kitchen, where he was told that his job was comparable to being given a ticket to hell. For security reasons, food preparation was closely scrutinized and mistakes were seen as attempts to compromise the inmates' safety. Six months into his term, he was transferred to the library for good behavior.

Michael Andropolis was sitting in the library reading Aristotle's *The Republic* the first time Malone saw him. A large man with broad, Aegean features, Andropolis wore standard tans and had his gray-black hair combed straight back on his head. As Malone pulled requested books for his mobile library rounds, Andropolis would stop reading, then quote the entire passage aloud, orating as if he were delivering a speech to a band of acolytes gathered on the Parthenon's east pediment.

Malone was reading one of his favorite authors, Stuart Woods, the next time he saw Andropolis. The older man was in the prison yard with his shirt off, sweating in the hot sun, dressing down another inmate for some karate exercise movement from which Andropolis had taken personal offense. Speaking forcefully but never once raising his voice, he had the other guy nodding and agreeing with everything he said.

"Hey, Fish!" Andropolis called, gesturing at Malone to come over and sit down.

Malone closed the book on a finger and walked out in the yard. He had learned early on when a stand-up guy beckons a new guy, known as a 'fish' to inmates, you went. At sixty-eight and with eight years of his sentence under his belt, Andropolis was among the higher, more respected ranks of the population. Malone had no qualms with the idea of getting on his right side, straight from the get-go.

"Mr. Andropolis," he said, nodding in deference. "How you doing, sir?"

"Hanging," Andropolis said. "Sit down here. You know anything about martial arts? Kumite?"

"Some. I studied it a couple years, back in the seventies."

Andropolis's face wrinkled in pleasure. "This clown's trying to tell me you move your whole shoulder when you throw a punch, like a boxer. I say that's all wrong. What do you say?"

Andropolis had just opened a door and invited him in.

"I was taught to keep your shoulders straight across your hips," he said. "You focus all your energy into your tsieken."

"What the hell is a seek-en?" the other guy asked.

Andropolis roared with laughter and waved a big fist in the guy's face. "That's your pile driver, chump!" he said, slapping him on the back. His eyes flickered from the guards around the yard up to the tower, making sure they knew he was being playful and not causing a problem.

The buzzer sounded the end of the exercise break. Still chuckling, Andropolis walked with Malone to the block entrance, then turned and stopped.

"I hear you got a degree in English," he said. "I like that. Yeah. I like that."

With that he walked away, leaving Malone standing in the yard and wondering what he had meant. His limited understanding of the prison's social system told him Andropolis had left the door ajar. Malone had passed inspection and he could now rightfully approach Andropolis with his head up.

Malone became fast friends with the older man over the months that followed. Trading favors when the need arose, they spent hours in conversations, about authors and their works, about composers and their music. Wiling away the interminable boredom ever present in confinement.

They trained together, learning the various Tai Kwan Do kumites from a picture book on karate. Before long, many of the inmates were working out with them, sweating and grunting behind prison walls in the hot sun.

Andropolis saved Malone's tail several times, dragging him away from toe-to-toes with a couple of the more radical inmates. Running interference with the guards. In return, Malone wrote down the man's musings, ordered books he wanted and generally became his right-hand man and personal aide.

As the days dragged by, Malone heard the usual stories: inmates claiming their innocence. Telling how they were set-up by overzealous or on-the-take cops, or how they happened to be in the wrong place at the wrong time.

Some stories he could believe, the obviously taller tales he could not. The stories that deeply disturbed him, though, were those involving fellow inmates' families.

The tendency in modern society is to throw things

away when they become old or damaged, whether it be clothes, cars, or televisions, even food. Families were abandoning relatives to prisons, jails, rest homes or— much worse—the streets. In doing so they were leaving behind irreversible social problems for their children and grandchildren to sort out, rather than taking a stand or doing the right thing.

Many of the inmates at the Pinellas County jail where Malone was incarcerated during his murder trial were there on serious charges, but most were not. The heavy hand of a state legislature populated with lawyers seeking to increase their personal wealth had come down.

The misnomered "people's representatives" had changed what were once merely citable misbehaviors into jailable offenses. Now white and blue-collar citizens were incarcerated for simple infractions, many of them absurd, victim-less peccadilloes. Law enforcement liked to call it public safety. Inmates called it "jack-boot" law.

Martin Craig was in the county jail with Malone. A tall, soft-spoken giant of an Irishman, Craig had related his dealings with the system to him as they talked one day on the cellblock.

"My family refuses to help me with my bond," Craig said, angry frustration growing in his eyes.

"How much is it?" Malone asked, pausing at his writing.

"Two hundred fifty dollars. They've blocked my calls, too."

"Did you write to anyone?" Malone asked.

"Yes, but they won't write back," Craig said.

Malone put down his pen and walked down the narrow gray corridor with Craig as he spoke of why he was there. He could not believe, yet instinctively did, what Craig told him.

Martin Craig had been stopped while riding a bicycle, and the arresting officer blow tested him twice. The result of each Breath-A-Lizer test was 0.02% blood alcohol level, well below the legal level.

But both tests were mistakenly recorded as one, at 0.22%. The legal limit in Florida was 0.08%. Craig had been arrested and in jail for five weeks already, for riding his bicycle after consuming one beer in the privacy of his own home.

Despairing inmates, Malone thought, thrown to the lions by their families. The great emperors of the American judicial system had given them a thumbs-down, while a comfortably numbed society looked away in ignorance and disgust.

* * *

Malone sat at the checkout desk in the library reading Henrik Ibsen's *Ghosts*. Michael Andropolis walked in, greeted Corporal Wilson at the door and sat down. He reached across and offered Malone his hand, looking at him like he was about to bust-out laughing.

"Way to go, man. You got your parole board hearing next week," he grinned. "Word is, they're going to let you fly."

Andropolis had pull, apparently far enough up the grapevine that he already knew the parole board's ultimate decision. Malone was not one to spit in fortune's face. If Andropolis had put himself on the line to find out, it was for real.

"I'm ready for it," he said. "Seventeen months and change and going out."

"Wish I could say that," Andropolis said. "I got another eight, ten years before they notice me, much less parole me."

"What was the name of that ship again?" Malone teased, Amazon Sky, or something like that?"

"Quit yanking my chain, Jazz," he laughed.

In May of 1988, Andropolis had been busted for masterminding a shipload of cocaine into St. Petersburg's Bayboro Harbor, then storing it in a warehouse in Tarpon Springs, Nine months later he got twenty-seven years.

"You got lucky on the murder count," Andropolis went on, "circumstantial evidence notwithstanding. But going down on trumped-up charges for smuggling a knife into the country doesn't make you any less a resident here than I am."

"Touché," Malone said. "But that's an issue I'm taking up with a certain John Tanner when I get out, if I can get to him."

Andropolis stared at him for a moment, then said, "I'm going to give you something—as a parting gift. What you do with it is your business."

He stood and walked to the shelves of books and scanned the titles. He looked over at the guard, then pulled out a small book that was pushed behind the rows and came back and sat down.

Wilson had his nose wedged in an Elmore Leonard novel and was lost to the world. Crime storywriters, Malone thought, could learn a few good lessons from Leonard's and Wood's work.

Andropolis opened the book and took out an onionskin that was tucked between the jacket and the back cover-leaf. He unfolded the delicate paper slowly, laid it on the desk and slid it across to Malone.

"All these names and numbers are up here," he said in a low voice and tapping his forehead, "I can use them anytime I want."

"What is this? Like a fail-safe?"

"In case anything happened to me while I was jacked in this place."

Andropolis rubbed his temples and closed his eyes as if meditating then let his breath out slowly.

"Believe me, Jazz," he went on wearily, "You're going to run up against people with power in places you never thought of. They know how to use it—and they will. They definitely will."

Over fifty names, the list was unbelievable. An unofficial registry of some of the biggest names in central and southeast Florida: judges, city officials, police, heads of federal agencies, bankers and lawyers. Not surprising, John Tanner's name was among them.

"Compiled that over the last eight years," Andropolis said.

"Kind of like a revenge list?"

"Yeah. When I took my fall, those guys were in there rooting for the feds. They were—and still are—just as guilty as I was."

Malone tucked the list in his pocket. "You mean the feds missed these people? They're still in business?"

"You kidding? Bigger and better than ever. With the Internet and cell phones advancing by light years? Government will never catch up. The peons are winning and Tanner's got big politicos working out of his pocket. How's that for chutzpah?"

"What better way to keep the spotlight off you?" Malone said. "I have to give him credit."

Andropolis stood up and stretched, then walked to

the shelf and put the book back in its place. He leaned down next to Malone and said, "Just remember the one worthwhile thing you keep quoting from that stupid little book of yours."

"Cover your ass," Malone said.

He winked before he went out, and said, "Come and see me after your hearing. Give the Redford boy a hug for me."

A cheap suit and tie, shirt, belt, shoes and socks, fifty bucks and a bus ticket back to St. Petersburg. The only thing Andropolis hadn't known was, this wasn't parole. The warden had maintained that Malone's sentence had been commuted to time served for good behavior.

The faceless person who had done this—or even why they had done it—was beyond Malone's scope. The wielders of power had somehow had his two-year probation waived, leaving him alone to face the lion's den when he returned to St. Petersburg.

15

After he got off the Greyhound bus in St. Pete, Malone took a taxi to an auto parts store, then to the storage facility. After putting a fresh battery in his truck, he drove to Ellen McVee's house in Clearwater. She was happy to see him.

Reddy took a running leap right through Ellen's screen door when he heard Frankenstein rumbling up the driveway. He ran to the truck, scrambled up through the window and landed sprawled on the seat. He gave Malone a tongue bath; slobbering all over his face and ears. One loud bark, then he sat twitching and quivering and mewling like a puppy.

Ellen stood by the driver's door, watching Reddy's antics.

"It's good to have you home, Jazz," she said, patting his arm. "I'm going to miss him."

She had tears in her eyes. Reddy had stolen her heart.

"Ellen, you have lifetime visitation rights," Malone said. "If anything like this ever happens again, you to take him for me permanently. Deal?"

"Okay, Jazz. It's a deal."

He looked at Redford, then the gaping hole in Ellen's screen door.

"Oh, don't worry about that old thing," she said, dabbing at her eyes with a small handkerchief. "I was going to have it changed anyway."

"Will you have dinner with me next week, Ellen? Maybe some sizzling souvlakia at Tsaliki's?"

"So many silly sibilants," she laughed. "Of course, Jazz, I'd love to."

Redford barked as they pulled away and Malone tooted the horn. Ellen waved, then went back inside. It had always been a mystery to him why some rich guy hadn't married her. She was a lady in the classic style.

Anxious to get home, Malone headed south on Bayview Bridge to Ulmerton Road, speeding down I-275 toward the looming dome of Tropicana Field. Parking by the curb at Mirror Lake he told Reddy to wait, then went inside to the condo office.

Mrs. Henderson, the resident manager, sneered as she handed him the passkey set. "Connie was here a couple months ago," she said. "Had an affidavit and a moving van. Cleared the furniture out of her ex-con, ex-husband's apartment in one fell swoop."

"Thank-you for sharing that with me, Mrs. Henderson," he said politely, then slammed the office door going out.

Redford jumped out of the truck and lifted his leg on the tire of a blue Toyota parked in front the truck. Malone remembered it was Mrs. Henderson's car.

"My sentiments, exactly," Malone murmured.

After parking in the garage, he rode the elevator to the eighth floor. When he opened the apartment door the ripe smell of dog drifted out. Mrs. Henderson was right— the place had been stripped. Clothes, books and manuscripts were scattered everywhere. He and Red would spend the night elsewhere and deal with it in the morning.

He left orders with the front desk at the Sahara Motel not to wake him for any reason. With Reddy sprawled beside him on an old lumpy mattress and all the lights on, he slept like a baby. The TV flickered in blue silence and the air conditioner ran full-blast all night.

* * *

It was still dark when Malone awoke. The LED's of the clock radio announced five a.m. He peered bleary-eyed out the window as some sadist with the St. Petersburg sanitation department backed his garbage scow up the alley, then repeatedly shook a dumpster he had suspended over the truck's dump well. Malone watched as the guy craned in the rear-view mirror and, using the big truck's hydraulic arms, tried to get a wet sheet of cardboard stuck to the dumpster's wall to drop out.

It was annoying, but after prison any sound reminding him he was back in the real world was worth it. He called Skyway Jack's on 34th street south, and ordered chop steak and eggs to go. Showering with Reddy, he used both bars of perfumed soap management had left on the vanity.

After breakfast, Reddy shredded a copy of the St. Petersburg Times Malone had read and handed to him by the section. Freedom was not just another word anymore.

At nine, Malone made calls. First to the power, phone, and cable companies, then he called Vern's office and made the required appointment with Lt. Cobb's secretary, Sissy, to see Vern that afternoon.

Fed, read, trucked, and…, Malone had forgotten the rest. Whatever it was, he was sure he and Redford hadn't had the pleasure in a quite a while.

A little after two he dropped Reddy off at the vet's for an exam, shots, and a manicure, then got caught in traffic on Ulmerton Road to the sheriff's offices in Largo. A rush of commercial vehicles, semis and transient snowbirds, making their way to and from the Gulf Beaches.

At a red light on the way, a tall, skinny guy with haystack hair stood on the middle island. Oblivious to the cars whizzing past on each side, he waved his arms as if conducting an orchestra. Malone shook his head and drove on, wondering what the world was coming to.

When Malone wheeled into the parking lot at the Sheriff's station and got out, an overweight sergeant eyeballed him as he walked toward the front doors. The sergeant had his officers lined up and dressed-out in full gear. While they stood at wary attention and sweating buckets in the hot, afternoon sun, he was doing a detailed inspection.

Malone waited for Lt. Cobb to escort him to his office. No longer classified as an upright citizen, he gazed half-heartedly at a glass and chrome display case in the lobby that stood beneath a wall-mounted American flag. There were trophies for championship bowling tournaments and softball leagues in the case. Numerous certificates and citations, for various community and charitable works, hung over them. Among the framed placards, he noticed, was an absorbing and revealing photograph.

In the photo, Sheriff Dodson was surrounded by the Citizen's Advisory Board while making a presentation to one of its members. The caption read: "John Tanner, President and CEO of Banco, C.A., and long-time, active board member, receives commendation from Sheriff Dodson for generous contributions to the Boys' and Girls' Ranches of Florida."

One of the double glass doors opened and Lt. Cobb walked out, jawing what appeared to be a whole pack of chewing gum, working it back and forth in his mouth. He had let his hair grow out somewhat and had it parted in the middle. He looked to Malone like he should have been wearing spectacles, bib overalls and holding a pitchfork.

Cobb stood beside him at the display case. "Beats hell out of a prison record, don't it, Malone?"

"What can I say? Prison time's not the end of the world."

Cobb nodded. "I got your paperwork on my desk. They couriered it over from Marianna. Clip this on your collar and let's get to it."

Handing him a visitor's pass, Cobb led the way around deputies manning the metal detectors. He pointed at the grids.

"We installed those last year. Some whacked-out druggy with a .22 hidden in his shirt blew holes in the walls. Scared the piss outta everybody."

Malone saw familiar faces on the walk to Lt. Cobb's office. He said hello to a few, but they ignored him. After years of dancing with lowlifes, he guessed, they could smell an ex-con.

Lt. Cobb sat down and shoved a pen and some papers across the desk. "Sit down, Malone, and sign these. You still report every thirty days 'til the end of your original sentence."

"I thought I didn't have parole? That's what the review board told me."

"It's not parole, the law requires it. We're supposed to keep an eye on you 'til you're flushed from the system."

"So, the system is just taking a dump where I'm concerned?"

"Watch your step, boy. You could get thrown back in that commode you just climbed out of."

"I'm not arguing with you, Vern. I still have a lot of questions about my arrest—and my early release."

Lt. Cobb leaned over the trashcan and launched the wad of gum into it with a loud thunk. "That's funny. I do too. Like what happened to the body for one thing."

"Your people dragged the lake," Malone said. "The assistant DA had the knife and Anne's dress. And what about the blood?"

"What good is blood if you don't know who it belongs to? DNA testing was done, but the DA really screwed up when he gave Williams the case."

Cobb stood up. "You want a cup of coffee?"

Malone followed him out to the coffee mess. "I thought torture went out with the dark ages."

Lt. Cobb rummaged through several file cabinets in the hallway. Malone stirred a heavy cream and sugar concoction into the burnt smelling, black liquid, then retreated to Vern's office to reconsider his coffee choice.

Cobb came back with a thick folder and plopped it on the desk and himself in the chair. He leafed through the contents, scratching his head and gruffing.

"I'm not supposed to do this, but I have an aversion to people getting railroaded. Something Williams submitted at the trial, before the bottom fell out. Admin… something. There has to be a copy of it here."

"Adminicular evidence," Malone said. "Black's

Law Dictionary defines it as auxiliary or supplementary evidence, presented to explain and complete other evidence."

"Where'd you pick that up?"

"There are some good jail house lawyers where I was."

Ah, here it is." He scanned the page, then passed it to Malone. "An affidavit."

The sworn statement supported the evidence given at Malone's trial. It related how the eyewitness had observed him leaving the scene of the crime, and how he had followed him and found him at the lake afterwards. It went on to state how the witness had seen Malone throw the knife in the lake, then Anne's dress, wrapped around a rock. How Malone had been acting wildly, and the blood on his clothes.

Anthony Amato had signed the affidavit. It was dated 12 July 2003—the fateful day at the cabin in Cove Cay.

"Something's wrong here," Malone said. "Tony was at the lake when I got there, waiting for me."

"That's not what he told me," Lt. Cobb said. "His sworn statement supported what he said were the way things happened."

"I have to get out of here," Malone said. His head was spinning and he felt the way he had that day at the lake, with Tony staring at him.

"Whatever you say, honch," Cobb said. "Give me a call later and we'll talk about it some more."

Malone tossed an idea around in his head as he drove home. He was having a conflict with something Lord Macaulay had said: "There is only one cure for the evils which newly acquired freedom produces; and that is freedom."

What was being passed off as freedom in this country was anything but. It had become big business, a system bloated with lawyers and legalese, hemorrhaging under the crushing weight of its own immoralities.

* * *

On the way to the veterinarian's Malone stopped and bought a cheap phone, an air mattress and a few bathroom supplies. By the time he and Reddy got back to the condo, the setting sun was painting the bare walls with blood-red slashes of color and the overhead lights were still on.

He opened the sliding doors at both ends of the apartment to let air flow through. The phone rang the moment he plugged it in. Strange, he thought, since no one knew his number had been reactivated. Lt. Cobb, Ellen, and the resident manager, were the only ones who knew he was home.

"Hello?"

"Jazz?" a woman's voice said. "Is this Jasper Malone?"

"Who is this?" A year and a half away from their games, he was in no mood to be pandered to by telephone salespeople.

"I just wanted to hear your voice," she said, her voice sounding distant and tired. "It's Anne, Jazz. I have to go."

"Wait, Anne!" he yelled.

A click. Silence.

She had come back.

16

When all the action is at the front door," Lt. Cobb said over the phone, "and you know you're not going to get in, no matter who invited you to the party, go around to the back door, Jazz. It's probably standing wide open."

"How does this relate to my situation?"

The moment Malone stretched out on the air mattress, Redford trotted over and laid across his back, like a sack of flour slung over a donkey. He wouldn't leave his master for a second, even when Malone sat on the porcelain throne.

"I get a call out of the blue from Anne, and you're telling me to go around to the back door?"

"It's obvious," Cobb chuckled. "Unless that was a very long-distance call, or say it really was Anne, you were set up. My first question at this point would be, who staged this whole thing? My second would be, why? What's their reason for investing that much time on you?"

"You forgetting something, Vern? I was there. Anne and I were the ones who got beat up. She disappears and I go to jail and then to prison."

"Didn't they teach you anything about smoke screens in the Navy?" Lt. Cobb said. "The little guy you told me about, the one that decked you? He had you looking one way and then got you from another."

"Diversionary tactics, plain and simple," Malone

said. "So, what's this got to do with front doors and back doors?"

"Aw, Malone. If you think Tanner is behind this like you claim, we both know he's got a lot to protect. He sure as hell isn't going to let you in the front door. From where I sit, it didn't matter one iota it was Anne who invited you in."

Malone hung-up, then carried the air mattress out on the balcony. The dog smell in the apartment had given him a headache, and the fresh air would be a nice change from the recycled night-gasses of seven hundred and fifty edgy inmates.

* * *

The sun slipped up over Tampa Bay and zephyrs of warm, Florida air whispered through the trees. In his first relaxed sleep in seventeen months and twenty-two days, Malone was slow in waking. Redford's insistent mewling and pacing were signs he had forgotten over the course of his absence that meant the boy had to go.

When he finally turned over and sat up, Red already had his leg lifted and was letting loose a pulsing stream through the guardrail. It disintegrated as it fell eight floors, and Malone was sorry for any pedestrians who may have happened by during those unfortunate moments.

He pulled on his clothes, then snapped the leash on Reddy and walked him two miles to the beachfront Sandwich Shak for croissants and coffee. He sat on a white patio chair and watched a rookie wind-surfer try to stay on his board long enough to catch a breeze.

He knew a direct assault on John Tanner was out of

the question. Tanner had too many layers of defense between himself and commoners like Malone. He had to find that back door, as Cobb had put it, starting over in a sense. Armed with the list Andropolis had given him, he would pick away at the imperfections in the banker's operations. His desire now was to render like for like and bring some measure of pain into Tanner's world.

Malone discovered at the bank later that Connie had tapped their joint accounts for everything, a total of seventy-eight thousand dollars. Aggravated, he cashed two bonds from his personal safety deposit box and headed for south St. Petersburg.

A grizzled, old used-furniture dealer he had done business with in the past, "Sarge" Jackson had just unlocked the front door and propped it open when Malone walked up and tapped him on the shoulder. Thin and wiry, his chocolate skin dried by the sun, Sarge's hair had turned pure white since their last meeting.

'Hey, you old fart!" Malone tied Red to the front door knob as Sarge spun around and squinted, then smiled. A cigarette dangled precariously from between his lips.

"Who you calling old fart, white boy? I ought to whip your tail up and down this block, show who's the old fart here!" He started laughing and coughing and the cigarette went flying out of his mouth.

"How you been?" Malone said. "It's been ages...."

"Getting by," he said. "Where's the missus today?" Sarge lit another cigarette, licked the filter, then pasted it in the corner of his mouth.

"Connie hit the road, months ago."

"She gots the furniture and you gots the shaft," Sarge laughed. "And you want me steal your money again, right?"

"Show me what you got. I need a house full."

"Well, come-on back to the warehouse, and let's see what I got I can off-load on you."

After looking over what Sarge called his new stuff, Malone picked the pieces he liked and told him where to deliver it, then handed him five crisp, one-hundred dollar bills. The old man beamed at him like he had been handed a bar of gold.

"I knew they was something I like about you," he said, counting out change. "No plastic, always pay cash. Stuff it in my pocket, keep it off the books, bank and tax vultures don't get they clutches on it. Who gonna be wiser?"

"I take it you don't like banks," Malone said.

"Never did," Sarge said, "specially not after what that son-of-a-bee-dog Tanner did to me. Him and that fancy lawyer he got——what's his name--Tomato or some crap or 'nother."

"You know Tanner? And Tony Amato?"

"Know them? Hell, I used to cook breakfast for them honkies, wipe they lily-white lips for them when they done."

Back in the showroom Sarge sat down in a Lazy-Boy and laid the chair back into a full recline. Malone sat in an armchair across from him and watched him light another cigarette with the previous one, then pinch out the butt between his fingers and drop it on the concrete floor.

"Bring your hound out' the sun," Sarge said. "Gots to be poking eighty-five out by now. I get Nan bring him some water."

When Nan brought the bowl, Redford lapped up the water. Lying down beside Malone's feet, he laid his head on his paws.

"I didn't know you were a chef," Malone said. "I had the impression you'd been in the furniture business for a while."

"Hell no, boy. I only been doing this," he said, hooking his thumb at the oddly assorted showroom, "going on five years now. Me and Nan had a restaurant. Nothing fancy, mind you, did a good bidness. Stuck half the till in our pockets every night, happy as flies on stink."

Malone had been good friends with Sarge for several years, but never knew his reasons for hiding his right hand in his pocket all the time. It became evident when he held it up.

"How many fingers you see? Gots to be four sisters and a brother to cook any good. He know Nan don't cook too good, so Tanner make damn sure I couldn't do it no more. Left me to spin like a windmill in the wind."

Sarge grinned through a cloud of smoke, showing crooked, nicotine-stained teeth. A thick, bright-pink scar where his index and middle fingers should have been crawled ugly and jagged to what little remained of his thumb.

"Tanner did that to you? Why?"

"He want me and Nan's restaurant. Call it an e'cellent tax shelter."

Sarge told him how Tanner had made quick and easy loans to the couple through his bank, helping them expand their business. When they started making good money, the banker offered to buy them out but they refused. Tanner sent one of his flunkies to chop Sarge's fingers off one night in the restaurant—with his own cleaver.

"I'm down, and he get Tomato to buy the mortgage!" Sarge said. "Then he call the note. Been washing his money since."

"How do you know he still owns the place?"

"That's easy, sonny. You go over to Sugar's any day 'round noon. His silver Lexus sitting out front? He be sitting inside in a back booth, talking on that portable phone he got, flapping his jaw with Tomato."

Old Sarge had just sold him a load of furniture, and in telling him about his personal encounter with implacability, had showed Malone the back door. If it were standing open, he knew he would need to enter with both eyes wide open. Starting his truck, Malone decided what a modern-day Junius would have said: "As for Mr. Tanner, there is something about him which even treachery cannot trust."

It took Malone a couple weeks to get the condo back into some semblance of order. After he repainted it, Sarge's furniture delivery made it look livable. He hung Mayan blankets, then lined what was left of his library on shelves made of pine planks and patio blocks. The stereo system arrived by delivery truck, so he played a Mozart CD, and humming along, felt respectable once again.

Keeping his distance, the following Tuesday Malone tailed John Tanner from his home on Snell Isle. Recording his movements and activities with a Nikon he had bought, he logged addresses and license-tag numbers at every stop. Despite his efforts to remain obscure, over the ensuing weeks Tanner became relatively definable and very predictable in his ways.

Even though Tanner could afford the best security money could buy, he apparently knew nothing about port-able phones' susceptibility to eavesdropping. Every stop including at Sugar's, he would leave his cell phone behind and go inside to talk on the portable house phone. After listening and recording Tanner's conversations over the scanner he had installed in Frankenstein, Malone saw a definite pattern beginning to emerge.

17

Malone was working on a short story about a New Age minister he had met while atop the sacred pyramid at Chitzen Itza. The setting sun glowed from behind a gold-fringed scattering of clouds while he wrote. He tried to ignore the phone's warbling tones, but the sounds bothered Reddy.

He got antsy and started growling at it. When it continued, he barked and nosed the receiver off the cradle. Malone retrieved it from the floor, muffled the mouthpiece and gave the boy a Bronx cheer. Reddy mistook it for an invitation to a kiss, and nearly knocked him over.

"Malone and Associates," he said. "You whack 'em, we stack 'em. Toe tags are extra."

"You take up a new line of work?" Lt. Cobb said. "Sounds like an advert for a Mafia-run funeral home."

"Sorry. I've gotten about three-dozen calls in the last week. Salespeople trying to convince me I need their junk."

"Try hanging up on them!"

"I do. I'm training my answering machine to do it too."

"I wanted to ask you something," Cobb said. "You ever do a follow-up on Mrs. Hunter?"

"I've been on temporary assignment, Vern. You know how sticky wardens are about inmates taking personal leave from their institution."

"I hear you. Looking through my notes back when I was tracking Gridley James, I called up there and asked the nursing facilities' administrator when I could send an officer up with a complaint form on Gridley James for the old lady to sign. She told me Mrs. Hunter had already been checked out."

"What happened to James anyway?" Malone said.

"Must have disappeared down the same hole he slithered up out of," Lt. Cobb said. "Know what's interesting about this Hunter thing? Tony checked her in. What makes it even more fun? She was checked out the day before we arrested you."

Malone played with the phone cord and debated whether to tell Cobb about the list he had gotten from Andropolis. Tanner had squeezed Tony and in turn Tony had squeezed him, both men trying to make a contraband dagger pop out.

"I need to get with you on something, if you don't have a problem with associating with ex-cons?"

"Like I told you before, man," Cobb said, "you looked pretty rough at the trial and your attorney kind of let the state then the feds roll right over you."

"A system without brakes," Malone said. "At least not for guys like me."

If he had been rich, things would have been different right from the start. The assistant DA's high aspirations had made his case pocket change, though.

"You want to know something else?" Lt. Cobb said, taking a deep breath. "The knife we dragged from the bottom of the lake? One the feds hung you with on the smuggling charge? I ran it through Jim Davis with U.S. Customs in Tampa. His report came back saying it was a registered import."

"Meaning?"

"It wasn't smuggled. It was imported legally."

"You let me sit in jail, for nearly a year and a half, holding the bag?"

"Wasn't my fault. Our department only collected the evidence," he said. "Ultimately, the feds presented it."

It was obvious, Malone thought. Knowing the process and probably already knowing the outcome, Tony had handed him off.

"So, I put it to you," Cobb said. "If these people can jug up the legal system so easily with private citizen Malone, what would they have done if I had gotten sucked into it?"

"Probably drawn and quartered you," Malone said.

"I don't need to tell you what they do to ex-law enforcement in the gray-bar hotel. Come down here sometime tomorrow, see what we can come up with."

"Why don't you meet me just off the corner of Fifth Avenue North and Thirty-Fourth street in St. Pete, around noon. I'll be parked across the street from a place called Sugar's. There is someone who stops there regularly I think you might be interested in."

"I know the place," Lt. Cobb said. "I'll be there about eleven-thirty. I got a court appearance downtown at one."

Malone was reading Stuart Woods' *Blood Orchid*, working the recorder and trying to edit Tanner's conversational breaks when an unmarked squad car pulled to the curb in front of his truck. He had hung a beach towel over the rear window to keep the blazing sun from frying his neck and took occasional gulps off a liter-bottle of Mountain Dew he kept packed in ice.

Lt. Cobb got out and the squad car pulled away. He held a bulging, grocery-size paper bag in one hand and jammed his Stetson on with the other. Opening the driver's door, he shoved the bag across the seat to Malone and climbed in.

"Hope you're hungry," he said. "I brought Chinese."

"Read my mind," Malone said. "Breakfast was a doughnut and three coffees. Which one's louder? My growling stomach or my screaming bladder?"

Cobb unloaded the bag on the seat. Quart containers of chicken chow mien and beef lo mien, napkins, plates, and plastic forks. Small bags of soy and mustard sauce. Desert was fortune cookies, a handful of them.

"You don't carry a bladder bottle?" he said.

"It's jammed behind the seat," Malone said. "Most times I aim it through that hole in the floorboard between your boots."

Lt. Cobb started in on the low mien beef and looked over the camera and electronics gear.

"Interesting little setup you got here," he said.

"The things you can learn with setups like this." Malone dribbled soy sauce on the chicken chow mien and began eating.

"Like what?" Lt. Cobb said, sucking up a low mien noodle.

"See that Lexus parked in Sugar's lot?" Malone pointed at a silver sedan. "That and the restaurant belong to John Tanner.

So? The man's got a sideline business, and doesn't drive a fancy car. Doesn't make him any more suspect than you or me."

Cobb swallowed the last few bites of his lunch, then opened a cookie and read his fortune.

"Yeah, my ass," he said, squinting at the ribbon of paper. "I'm going to receive a large inheritance."

"You should be so lucky," Malone said, dropping his empty carton in the paper bag. "You remember Michael Andropolis? The Bayboro Harbor bust in eighty-eight?"

"Jungle Mike? The Greek cocaine cowboy they called him," Cobb said, munching cookie pieces. "All over the news."

Tanner's telephone started transmitting and the scanner, on sweep select, locked on the signal then pumped his voice over the speakers. Malone keyed the recorder and Cobb leaned forward over the steering wheel, listening intently.

A heavily-accented man named Ramirez spoke with Tanner about a shipment of antiques from South America. They discussed departure and arrival dates, then arranged to meet later at Tanner's bank to iron out details. When they hung-up, the scanner fell silent, its LED's indicating it was once again sweeping the bandwidth.

"I gotta git," Lt. Cobb said, looking at his watch, "Tell me what you got while I drive this thing over to the county courthouse."

He started the truck, then burned the tires pulling away from the curb. Cobb wove through traffic at a dizzying pace, driving like he was behind the wheel of an official vehicle instead of a beat-up, Chevy truck.

"Andropolis gave me a list. Among others, John Tanner's name is on it." Malone took out his notebook and photo collection and showed him the pictures and notes he had made on Tanner's activities.

"He spends most of his day in his car, on his cell phone or visiting his various business interests, setting up what seem to be some kind of deals. A friend of mine, Sarge Jackson, said your upright citizen is funneling money through Sugar's. Used to be his restaurant before Tanner's bank foreclosed on it."

"Naturally," Cobb looked at Malone through the corners of his eyes. "If Mr. Jackson has his facts straight, it's likely Tanner is laundering funds through his other interests too."

"And leaving a long paper trail."

Lt. Cobb pulled over at the courthouse promenade on First Avenue, then got out. He walked around the truck, then leaned down and gave Malone a wary look. "I'm worried about you, boy. You got yourself messed up with Tanner once before and look where it got you. I was you, I'd back off a little, let me check some things before you get bit again."

"Make a deal with you," Malone said, sliding behind the wheel. "Take a closer look at Tanner, run these license plates for me, and I'll take a closer look at Tony in the meantime."

"Bound to work," Cobb said, "but watch your step with Tony. If he's in Tanner's pocket, the same bottom feeders are working for him as for our banker buddy."

"I'll keep it in mind."

Malone tooted the horn as he pulled away. Cobb waved, cocked his hat at a just-so angle, then swaggered up the walkway to the county building and the courtrooms.

Later that evening, Malone was craving a Polish

sausage and a beer, and waded down the beach in the surf wash with Redford to the Sandwich Shak. A full moon lit the clear waters of a tidal basin near the Pier. The ghostly form of a manta ray winging its way about in pursuit of tiny morsels cast eerie patterns against the shallow bottom sands. Each time the ray changed directions, Reddy turned with it and growled low at the mystic shape, as if he were luring it closer, trying to import the purpose of this strange creature.

Malone walk out to the end of the Pier's concourse and sat inside one of the short archways penetrating the guard walls all around, with his legs dangling over the side of the concrete and steel isthmus. The brown mustard and sausage tasted succulent and peppery and the Molson's was tangy and cold.

Soothed by the sounds of an incoming tide and the vast blackness of night with its ever-watchful eyes, for the moment Malone was at complete peace. Reddy nosed his way around to the various lamp-lit night fishers, looking for handouts and pestering the pelicans that sat nervously atop barnacle encrusted pilings, scolding him with Jurassic voices.

One footstep, just behind Malone. The click of a safety, and a cool, hard cylinder pressed against his neck.

"Move over," a man's voice whispered, as he lowered to one knee and leaned close. "This is a silenced, nine-millimeter against your head, with a full clip of metal jackets waiting to make fish food out of your brain. You'll be dead, and I'll be gone before anyone realizes it was anything more than a can of beer being opened. Nod if you catch my drift."

Malone carefully nodded once, fearful of the finger that weighed his life in the balance. Redford was dancing in the shadows further down the pier, too far away to be of any help.

"People I work for asked me to chat with you," the man's whisper went on. "They're remorseful you didn't give up your sleuthing, especially after demonstrating their dissatisfaction several times. Keep your eyes straight ahead."

He felt the gun barrel slide around his neck, then caught a glimpse of a tall figure sitting down next to him in the opening and dangling his legs through. The man pushed his pork pie hat further down on his forehead and clapped his arm around Malone's shoulders like an old friend, then pressed the gun in his ribs.

"Just so we're on the same page," he said in a low voice. "You had your chance. I'm here to insure it won't happen again."

He unbuttoned his shirt, pulled a manila envelope out, then opened it. Sliding the contents out onto his lap he flashed Malone's pictures and notes, tossing them into the bay, then following them with his tapes.

"Stand up, Malone," he said quietly. "We're going to take a little ride. You with me so far?"

"Not willingly."

Tall Paul pocketed the gun and lowered one hand to the concrete deck then grasped at a railing with the other. Bracing himself awkwardly, he scooted back far enough to slide his legs out to rise. It was all the time Malone needed.

He grabbed the rail and kicked his feet out, then knifed through the small opening like a log spearing off a cliff. He hit the water feet first and plunged below the surface. The first bullet sluiced past him in the water, then two more followed in rapid succession.

Malone swam underwater toward the pier pilings. Slowly surfacing, he treaded water backwards until he was sure he was out of the shooter's line of sight. Redford barked continuously from somewhere above. The people standing at the rail were yelling and pointing down the pier, but no more bullets hit the water.

18

There were times when unknowns would nearly immobilize him, times Malone couldn't quite overcome obstacles life had placed in his path. Sometimes it was just writing a difficult passage of fiction, or resolving the seemingly insurmountable problems importing Mayan goods would create.

He would retire to his study, light a candle and turn off the lights, then meditate, gazing at the flame for hours. His mind would settle, his body would release its tensions and the framework of a plan would emerge.

The candle had burned down to a puddle and light was squeezing through the blinds when Malone realized what his efforts were lacking. Like Mrs. Hunter, he needed to give form to his fears. That meant confronting John Tanner, something he felt he might accomplish obliquely through Tony.

He called Ellen McVee and had her make a lunch date with Tony for him at the Little Italy on Forty-Ninth Street. Then he told Lt. Cobb about the run-in at the pier and asked him for the number of the import record and the name of the customs agent he had dealt with in Tampa. Cobb groused about private detectives, but gave him the details and hung up.

A light rain was falling as he and Redford left Mirror Lake. The clouds had cleared and the sun was humidifying the air to steam bath consistency when they arrived at the stud service appointment in High Point.

A ten-mile, twenty-minute trip turned into an hour of sitting in a line of cars waiting to pass through a gamut road construction barricades had created. A husky woman wearing an orange safety bib and an attitude was directing traffic, looking as if she ate rhinoceros for breakfast then picked her teeth with the bones.

A neighborhood eatery, Little Italy was noisy, with imitation grapevines hanging over the pastoral, Italian murals adorning its walls. Pizza and beer fanatics occupied its small booths, and it was busy—in case Tony decided to bring reinforcements.

A copy of the customs report lay on the table next to Malone's cheesy-tomato pizza and pitcher of beer when Tony walked in alone. He was pale and drawn and his suit needed pressing and worry lines etched his forehead.

Malone pulled a slice loose and dropped it on a paper plate, then pushed it over to Tony as he slid into the booth. Tony sat for a minute surveying the pizza like it was a UFO meal tray, then frowned.

"Are you wired, by any chance?" he said.

"Why would you ask me that?" Malone said. "Should I be?"

"What do you want, Jazz?" Tony said. "You must know you're jeopardizing my position by meeting like this, considering my current business client obligations."

His eyes darted around the restaurant as he wound strings of cheese around his finger. He looked tired and discouraged.

"That cheese is like the mess you've involved me in," Malone said. "Just when you think you've wrapped it up, another loose string shows up."

"You don't know the half of it. There are some serious players in this mess as you call it."

Tony resorted to cutting his pizza with a fork, angrily spearing the pieces and chewing.

"You know what this is?" Malone asked, spinning the report around.

Tony studied it as he chewed, more irritated than surprised. "It's a copy of an import registration," he replied, pouring himself a glass of beer. "For the dagger you were supposed to recover. So what?"

"Then neither you or Tanner were really interested in finding Mrs. Hunter. Just a contraband dagger."

Tony looked nonplussed. "Esther had the unfortunate luck of being in the right place at the wrong time."

"The right place because...."

"The dagger was brought in with other registered artifacts to the antique store where she happened to see it and buy it."

"And the wrong time?"

"The real dagger was supposed to be brought to Tanner personally. It was accidentally sold before he could give specific instructions for delivery."

"Let's see if I've got this straight," Malone said. "Tanner registers an artifact for importing, substitutes a contraband dagger, then loses it in the shuffle at the antique store? Doesn't that, like, make you an accessory in a federal way?"

"You win the stuffed monkey," Tony said, smearing rings of water on the table with his finger. "Knowing how he did it, though, and proving it are two different things. Even if you knew where the dagger is— what's the word of a convicted felon worth?"

"So there's no foreign client waiting anxiously for the return of a priceless artifact?"

"No, but the reward still stands if you're interested."

The temptation to mention Vern's growing interest in the oddities surrounding Tanner's activities was almost too much for Malone to bear. His uneasiness with Tony's condescending tone and his proximity to a source related to his problems gave him pause to reconsider the timeliness of such a revelation.

"You know anything about a guy named Gridley James?" he said. "Or where I might find him?"

The corner of Tony's mouth twitched. "Only that he's a relative of Mr. Tanner's who does odd jobs for him."

"Jobs like trashing Mrs. Hunter's property? Jobs like beating her up when she got in the way of Tanner's locomotive?"

"I wouldn't know anything about that."

"I'll bet. Are you aware that it was James who broke her arm, right before he checked her into that nursing facility?"

Tony looked shocked, but neatly avoided the question.

"I'm responsible for her well-being if mental incapacitation occurs. Which it had."

"So you knew where she was all along," Malone said. "Who checked her out the day before my arrest?"

"I have no idea," he said, not looking up. "I authorized her admission with administration at Seven Sands. What happened after… that I'm not sure."

Tony's cell phone interrupted. He turned away to answer it, speaking short words in a low voice, watching

Malone. He hung up, then dropped the phone in his coat pocket.

"Duty calls," he said. "We finished?"

It was a statement more than a question. He was obviously evading, but the cat and mouse routine had elicited much more information than Malone had expected.

"Tell me something," Malone said, wiping his hands with paper napkins and throwing them on the pizza remains. "How does Tanner find time for his bank with all these sideline things?"

"A rich man? With a staff of experts capable of handling anything that comes up at the bank?" Tony said. "I'd say he can oversee his enterprises in whatever manner he sees fit."

"With enough muscle to squeeze guys like me. Trying to prevent anyone from figuring out when, where, and how he does it, right?"

"You could say that," Tony smirked. "But we prefer to call it insurance."

"Right. One of his insurance agents tried to cancel my policy last night," Malone said. "I may be a little guy in Tanner's grand scheme of things, but that doesn't give him the right to walk all over me."

"I'll see what I can do," Tony said, standing and brushing crumbs off his suit. "Next time you invite me to lunch, make it a place where they have a wine list and real napkins."

Malone grabbed his sleeve as he moved away. "One more question before you take off. Do you know where Anne is?"

His eyes turned mean. "Anne is no longer a problem," he said, yanking free and walking away.

As Malone paid the check, Tony stood beside his Mercedes in the parking lot talking heatedly with a tall guy wearing a pork-pie fishing hat and chartreuse-rimmed sunglasses. Getting in Tony's face, he jabbed a finger hard into his sternum.

Tony yelled something at him, then got in his car and tore away. Peering in Malone's direction through the glass window, the tall guy pointed at him, then turned and walked down the shopping center.

* * *

The federal building in downtown Tampa was an ominously quiet place on any day of the week. Many of the staff officers and clerical personnel had taken an extended Easter weekend. The freezing air conditioning, combined with the absence of regular workaday sounds and people moving about the hallways made it seem like catacombs in the dead of winter.

Malone found U.S. Customs on the lobby directory, then climbed the stairs to the fourth floor. When he asked the sole duty clerk for Jim Davis's office, he was led down a carpeted hallway straight to his door.

With a picture of President Bush looking over his shoulder, Jim Davis sat at his desk. The desktop was covered with a sheet of clear glass, and had a large calendar blotter placed squarely in its center. Pressed under the glass and arranged neatly around the calendar were his various schedules, memos and letters. The only other work tools on the desk were a computer terminal, and a black, government-issue pen next to it.

Davis wore a white short-sleeve shirt and tie, his ruddy features topped by bushy eyebrows and unruly black hair. The black, horn-rim glasses were a throwback to the sixties, and looked too small for Davis's face.

"Have a seat, Mr. Malone," Davis said, glancing out the window at the thunderheads billowing far out over the Bay. "Looks like we're going to get dumped-on."

"Typical for this time of year," Malone said. "Appreciate your sticking around, with the egg bunny on his way."

"No problem. I'll make this as brief as possible," he said. "I talked to Lt. Cobb, and he told me about your case."

Davis opened his desk and took out a manila folder. Removing the contents, he spread them out over his desktop, and then sorted them.

"These are selective copies of various agency reports related to recent customs' surveillance and federal investigations. All have either a direct or an indirect bearing on your investigation."

He separated a document and looked at Malone. "We will require a signed secrecy oath from you if you want information related to our operations."

"Why all the secrecy? I thought this was just an ordinary, everyday case of smuggling?"

"There are no ordinary, everyday cases of smuggling, Mr. Malone."

Davis handed Malone his pen, then laid the form in front of him. Davis waited patiently while he signed, then quickly scooped up the paper and slipped it into in the folder.

"We're working with the FBI and the DEA on the this one," he said. "We have reason to believe that John Tanner has direct links to organized drug-smuggling."

"You mean like the Cali cartel type of drug

smuggling?"

Davis loosened his necktie and unbuttoned the collar, then leaned back and grinned like a Cheshire cat. "Not like the Cali cartel...."

Malone was stunned.

"Knowing that doesn't help me any. His people already tried to splash my gravy several times."

"We're aware of that," Davis said. "I'll put you in touch with FBI Special Agent in Charge, Daryl McFarland—goes by Mac. He'll brief you on what's needed. Nothing risky on your part, just stay on the sidelines and try not to interfere."

Davis led him down the hallway. At the front desk he turned, then stretched and yawned.

"The only thing our agency will want from you," he said, "is a periodic report about the nature of any contacts you may have with Tanner's organization. That includes Anthony Amato."

A powerful storm wreaked havoc on the night, blistering the air with intense, jagged streaks of lightning. Malone pulled his air mattress over by the east balcony and put Beethoven's Moonlight Sonata on the CD player. Sitting safely behind the sliding glass doors, he sipped a beer and watched ribbons of white fire jump between thick banks of clouds hovering low over a turbulent bay.

He missed his bulldog, away with his lady-friend for the night. He missed Anne terribly, wishing she would show up on his doorstep once again, but knowing painfully it was unrealistic.

What had soured him over the last few months was, for the longest time he had thought of Tony as his friend.

He also had considered himself at odds and constantly on the defensive those rare times in the past when he had encountered Vernon Cobb.

Now, just the opposite was becoming evident. While a little sooner would have been nice in the scheme of things, Malone realized Lt. Cobb had gone to bat for him and had, as his baseball-loving Aunt Mildred used to say, put one in the strawberry patch. There was a lot more to the Florida cracker than Malone had given him credit for.

Cobb had become his friend at a time when everyone else had given him up for lost.

19

The phone jarred Malone out of an uneasy sleep, and he rolled off the air mattress and stumbled to the kitchen in a fog. He wasn't happy about calls that came before some caffeine had made its way into his brain.

"Malone and Associates," he said. "This better be good."

"Jasper Malone?" a gravelly voice said. "This is FBI Special Agent in Charge, Daryl McFarland. Jim Davis gave me your number; said I should call you. Didn't wake you, did I?"

"No, I had to get up to answer the phone," he said, clearing his throat. "What do you need?"

"A meeting," Agent McFarland said. "You and Lt. Cobb and me, ASAP. How about ten, at his office? He knows we're coming."

Malone squinted at his watch. It was nine a.m.—on a Saturday morning.

"Well, Special Agent in Charge Daryl McFarland, I haven't had coffee yet," he grouched, "much less gotten dressed."

"Call me Mac. I've got it covered, Malone. I'll spring for doughnuts and coffee, you just be there, dressed and ready to dig in. We have a lot to cover."

He hung up before Malone could say yea or nay. Free doughnuts and coffee though, and the feds were buying.

Malone threw on jeans, a T-shirt and sandals, ran a comb through brown tangles of hair, then hit I-275 towards the St. Petersburg-Clearwater airport doing sixty-five. The steering wheel shimmied all the way.

How things had changed at the sheriff's department since his last visit. Walking through the lobby, Malone looked at the display case where Tanner's picture was displayed.

He felt an immediate and smug degree of satisfaction when he noted someone had removed the photo and the certificates commending Tanner's contributions. The Police Benevolent Association no longer wanted his drug-subsidized gifts, it seemed, nor his image staining their prized trophy case.

The security officer gave Malone a visitor's pass, no questions asked.

It was feeding time at the Pigs 'R' Us freebees rally in Lt. Cobb's office. The lieutenant, two deputies, and another man Malone didn't recognize were taking turns attacking the doughnuts. They were circling the box of sweets like wolves, sipping large cups of Starbucks' coffee.

"Stout, you and Robbins clear out of here," Lt. Cobb said, licking his fingers and scoping-out the chances of a replay. The two officers left and Malone sat down, ruefully eying the remaining doughnut choices.

"Mac, this is Jasper Malone," Lt. Cobb said. "Grab it and growl Jazz or there isn't going to be anything left to grab."

Cobb lifted out a powdered bun that was stacked high on one end with vanilla crème. He winked at

Malone, then took half the doughnut off in one chomp, savoring the rich filling.

Malone took a chocolate-glazed doughnut and tapped himself a cup of coffee from the Starbucks urn. Standing near the door, he ate slowly as he traded stares with Special Agent-in-Charge, Daryl McFarland.

McFarland was wearing a gray, pinstriped suit, with a red-paisley tie and matching suspenders, and was balanced adroitly on a stool next to Lt. Cobb's desk. He had gelled red hair parted on the side and combed in closely regulated strokes. His suit coat hung open, and the butt of a gun protruded from an under-arm harness.

"Hear you spent some time at our fine facilities in Marianna," McFarland said, clapping his hands and dusting powdered sugar off his lapels. "For smuggling a contraband dagger or something like that?" He took a sip of coffee, nailing Malone with his eyes, telling him he didn't take to the idea of being in the same room with an ex-con.

"Something like that," Malone said, disliking him instantly. "I understand you people have known about Tanner for quite a while. Could have prevented my taking the trip in the first place."

"That's the way it goes," McFarland said. "When you're trying to pull in the big ones, you don't worry about little ones getting stuck in the net along the way."

"Are you saying the feds planned it that way?"

Lt. Cobb's eyes were going back and forth between them, like he was watching a tennis match. Munching his doughnut, sipping his coffee, and snorting softly. Getting a charge out of their exchange.

"Don't get your panties in a knot, Malone," McFarland said, sitting straight up on the stool. "We have an ongoing investigation and we're not about to compromise the whole operation for the likes of you. Who the hell do you think you are, anyway?"

"I'm a freeborn, tax-paying citizen just like you, is who I am," Malone said loudly. "Then again, I don't expect a tunnel-vision, thick-skinned government voyeur like you to have much training in protecting constitutional rights."

"All right, you two," Lt. Cobb finally said. "Enough with the penis banging. We got better things to do." He picked up his phone and punched in a number. "Harry? Cobb here...We're ready for you. Will you bring a Magic Marker along with you...Yes sir, everybody's here. Thanks, Captain."

Tall, burly and stone-faced, Captain Tate came in and sat down. McFarland nodded, then took the marker from him and moved over to the strategy board. He drew a line diagram, and labeled the branches with names matching the list Andropolis had given Malone almost to the person. Putting Tanner's name at the top, he wrote Cali cartel in a block over that.

"This is where we are in our investigations. Any questions?" he said, drilling Malone.

Lt. Cobb whistled through his teeth. "Looks like you folks got half the bigwigs in Florida tagged."

"A lot of man-hour intensive efforts have gone into this," McFarland said. "We can't afford the smallest mistake if we intend to bring this operation to a head."

"How'd you uncover the extent of their organization?" Malone said, looking for acknowledgement. "Only a well-placed source or intensive surveillance could collect that many names."

McFarland rolled his eyes, like he had just been

asked the price of a one-dollar cigar. "Malone, we've monitored their phones, their bank accounts--we can even tell when they use the toilet. Their supposedly secret meetings? We even taped them. We have prima facie evidence that will put the majority of the kingpins away—for a long time."

No acknowledgement would be made, Malone realized. When it came to resolution of federal cases, only agency insiders stood in the limelight. He and Lt. Cobb would not share the stage.

Captain Tate cleared his throat, then said, "How does our department fit into this operation, Special Agent McFarland? I'm sure Sheriff Dodson would be interested in your answer, not to mention my officers."

Lt. Cobb glanced over at Malone, wiggling his eyebrows, telling him to ask.

"Where do I hang on this tree, McFarland?" Malone said. "I went down for something having nothing to do with me and everything to do with Tanner."

"I'll get to you, Malone. Let me answer the Captain first."

McFarland turned back to the board and put asterisks next to a dozen or more names on the upper branches of the tree diagram. Malone recognized them as well-known municipal judges, rich, prominent attorneys, port authorities, and superintendents. Several of Florida's state and county regulatory agencies' enforcement divisions in and around the Tampa Bay area were listed.

"Captain Tate," he said. "The names I've noted are all at the state or local level and technically within the mandate of your authority. Hence, any arrests made and charges lodged will begin with the respective law enforcement agencies, which is your ballgame, sir."

"Thank-you, Special Agent McFarland," Captain Tate said. "The sheriff will be pleased to know this is a cooperative effort and not the normal steam-rolling the federal government is commonly known to effect."

McFarland looked ready to blow from the ears. Biting off a response to the Captain's remark he glared at Malone, then sipped his coffee and turned back to the board.

"There's a major flaw in your case, Malone," he continued. "We know now you were set up regarding the murder charge and the smuggling charge that followed. The flaw lies firstly with attaching a specific body to a specific murder, and secondly with locating the missing dagger."

He wrote Malone's name as a sub-branch of Tony's line, connected it to Tanner's, and drew a circle around all three, dividing their names from the rest. He shook his head, then glanced at Lt. Cobb.

"If you'll recall, a moment ago I said we could take down the majority of the kingpins. Our evidence on John Tanner is not sufficient at this time to complete our case against him."

Lt. Cobb looked as flabbergasted as Malone felt.

"You mean to tell me," Lt. Cobb said, his face turning red, "with all the fancy footwork your people have been doing, you still can't bring Tanner down? What's wrong with this picture?"

"If you'll give me a chance, Lt. Cobb, I'll explain," McFarland said. "As I said, we need a body and sufficient evidence linking John Tanner to that body. And we need the dagger. With justifiable cause—the body and the dagger—we can bring his whole house tumbling, with him at the bottom."

"I'll leave the details to you, Lt. Cobb," Captain Tate said, standing up. "I'll be in the sheriff's office this morning if you need me. Thanks again, Special Agent McFarland."

McFarland looked at his watch and said, "I've got another meeting with Jim Davis. You know where to find me, Lt. Cobb."

"Comprende," Lt. Cobb said.

McFarland picked up his briefcase and considered Malone for a few moments.

"Don't take it personal, Malone. Sometimes guys like you get the raw end of the stick in these matters. It serves no purpose to go off half-cocked, acting the indignant citizen."

"You suggesting I bend over and grab my ankles while federal dick-heads like you screw me over again?" Malone said. "Don't expect me to drop my pants for the likes of you, pal."

McFarland moved toward him with fire in his eyes, ready to throw a punch. Lt. Cobb grabbed his arm and shoved him toward the door, then out, saying he would call him later.

"I keep saying it, Jazz," Lt. Cobb said, coming back and sitting at his desk. "You aren't going to get in the front door, not with that temper."

"I know it," Malone said. "There's got to be an end to this somewhere. I'll be damned if I can see it just now."

"Take some time off, go someplace different for a couple days. Maybe I'll have something to run with when you get back."

"Can I take that as an official parolee directive?"

"Get out of here," he laughed. "Consider yourself

reported for thirty days. Things won't fall apart while you're gone."

Malone drove through a tangle of traffic on Ulmerton Road to the breeder's compound in Highpoint. After picking up Redford he headed north on the Bayview Bridge toward the lake.

He wanted to smell the air, wade in its tea-brown waters, and feel the warmth he and Anne had shared one night so long ago. Maybe the sweetness of her memory would wash away some of the hopelessness he had felt since that night in her apartment.

As he slowed for the off-ramp, Malone saw a green Porsche with the T-tops open flash past on the southbound bridge. A woman with her hair pulled back was at the wheel, speeding away in the southbound lanes.

He ran the red light at the foot of the ramp, gunned it going back onto the bridge, and accelerated until he was pushing seventy. Half a mile ahead, the Porsche wove through slower traffic the way Anne used to do, something he couldn't do in his old truck.

She was getting away. Malone was frustrated and angry. She was the only woman he had ever completely loved. The only woman he would have given his life to, had she wanted it.

20

For some people, getting away from it all involves weeks or even months of planning. Working out the smallest details, they fret with how to pack all that stuff in the car.

Even when they're on the road or at their vacation spot, they worry. About whether they sent the wormer medication along with the dog to the mother's. About whether all the lights were turned off or the doors were all locked. They never stop to consider the fact that, despite all their worry and agonizing, nothing really matters.

The sum of Malone's planning consisted of packing a clean shirt and briefs, his toothbrush, sandals and writing pads into his backpack, then loading the Redford-jet into the truck and hitting the road. He had learned from Reddy that, night or day, anywhere outside the apartment was a vacation and only the essentials were necessary. For Red, a leash. For him, a couple of articles of clothing. For both of them, instant freedom.

As with all the other holidays, Easter had become too commercialized for his tastes. Lacking significant replenishment for his soul, it usually came and went like any other day of the week. He had read about the upcoming Green Corn Festival in the Sunday paper, and decided the annual Miccosukee gathering would be a fitting place to recoup spiritual sensibilities.

When the alarm chimed Monday morning it was still dark. A crescent moon hung over the lighted crown of the Don Cesar far off in the west, glowing in muted splendor and looking like a cradle for a band of wing-weary, slumbering angels.

Malone drank in air, purified over the depths of the restless expanses of the Gulf, wafting in through the open windows. He made a pot of coffee, then took Redford out for his morning ritual.

As he drove around the cypress stands that crowded the edges of Lake Panasoffkee along U.S. Highway 41, the number of animal carcasses lying smeared across the road dismayed him.

Encroaching developments along Florida's coastlines were pushing the original inhabitants, including the Seminole and the Miccosukee, deeper into the outback and forcing them to live closer together, and ultimately nearer the brink of extinction. All in the name of a progress defined by entrenched politicians and intemperate corporate executives looking to satisfy their bottomless greed.

A small, hand-lettered sign directed Malone to a clearing off the main road. Wisps of smoke rose over the treetops, carrying the delicious aromas of pine-wood fires, roasting corn, and fish frying in garlic butter. He parked next to a row of cars, most of which had seen better days. Reddy jumped through the passenger window opening and ran to join a group of men dancing in circles around the ceremonial fire. The rhythms of two large, deep-throated drums throbbed from the perimeter.

Several of the men had on beaded headbands, with

cotton tee shirts and jeans, and wore moccasins that softened the staccato beat of their steps. A man with broad shoulders and high features, his hair falling in long, dark strands down his back, squatted and hugged Redford as if greeting a long-lost friend. Reddy slathered his face and yipped.

"My friend," he said, holding his hand out to Malone and beckoning. "Is this happy spirit your companion?"

"That he is," Malone said. "His name is Redford, mine is Jasper Malone."

He gripped Malone's hand firmly and stood gazing deep into his eyes, as other imposing braves danced past them. "I am Leon Grey Squirrel, Jasper Malone. Redford's presence here at this moment is a blessing to our people. We are honored you brought him to our celebration of the corn."

He turned to the dancers with arms raised, and shouted several words in the Seminole tongue, bringing the entire conclave to silence. Raising his face and hands to the sky, he spoke reverently, then directed all attention to Redford. He spoke to the dog, addressing him by name, then repeated the name to the members who gathered around them.

When he finished, he let out a rending yell and the drums and movement began again. All the men whooped and whistled, then joined the circle for the dance. Reddy sat there watching, flipping his head back and forth, licking their hands as they passed by. Each man in turn patted him gently.

Leon Grey Squirrel broke away from the circle as he neared where Malone stood and laid a hand on his shoulder.

"Our warriors dance in the way our fathers danced and in the way their fathers danced before them. If you are a warrior, then you would honor us with your dance, Jasper Malone."

A Miccosukee brave emerged from one of the canvas tents pitched further back from the ceremonial ring. He was dressed in a leather, range-rover's hat and jeans. His denim jacket was covered with infantry campaign patches and medals from several different Desert Storm combat theatres. His black hair was long and thin, flowing like silk strands around gaunt cheekbones as he walked.

"Well, I'll be damned!" he grinned. "If it isn't the old deck-swabber himself, Jazzbo Malone."

"You know our guest, Travis?" Leon Grey Squirrel asked.

"Sure do, uncle," he said, pumping Malone's hand enthusiastically. "Me and Jazz met up in Hawaii when I was on the way to the Mekong Delta back in '68. That was right before one of this squid's spy boats, the USS Pueblo, was captured off the coast of Korea."

"How you been, Raintree?" Malone said. "Is it true that the only way the Marines could get you to leave the jungle was to bag and tag you?"

Travis laughed long and hard. "Hey! I'm still walking around in this ungodly world, ain't I? No worse for the wear!" He looked Malone up and down, then said, "But you. You could use something from uncle's medicine bag."

Leon Grey Squirrel squinted at Malone, taking measure of his eyes and face.

"I can see you have the spirit of a warrior, Jasper Malone," he smiled. "Maybe a little weakened by your unhealthy ways, but still a well-proven one. Will you join with our brothers in the circle?"

"Of course he will, uncle," Travis said, grabbing Malone's arm and pulling him toward the festivities, "even if I have to drag him around it myself."

It took Malone three rounds to manage a lame imitation of Travis's quick foot movements, regulated by the drum beats in short, successive steps.

As they danced, the braves formed a line radiating out from the center of the circle. They draped their arms across each other's shoulders and swept slower dancers off to the sidelines.

Sitting on one of the logs that formed the outer ring, Malone was glad in a way. Their unrelenting pace had worn him out.

Reddy had wandered off to one of the white field tents, where a young woman kneeled beside him, petting him as he drank water from a yellow plastic bowl. Garbed in a multi-hued dress much like the one Malone's fourth-grade teacher had worn, she had a lock of black hair over her ear interwoven with a strip of leather, then braided tightly around a single feather. She lifted her head as if listening, then stood and opened the flap of the tent and motioned to someone inside.

A tall, strikingly handsome tribesman emerged and stood before the tent, looking out over the proceedings. He had a simple, woven cap on his head and a beautifully beaded, leather breastplate across his chest He wore pure-white, cotton slacks and matching vest over a silk, blouse-sleeved shirt. He held a large bouquet of green corn stalks in one hand and a ceremonial knife in the other. The knife's handle was wrapped in strips of alligator hide, and hung sheathed from his breechcloth.

When the other warriors saw him coming out they waved the drums silent. Suddenly, all of them began half-yodeling cries, then waved at him and exulted him to come out.

The women and children, the young and old alike, rose from beneath the shade of oak trees scattered around the clearing, then stood behind the men who had formed two ranks, one to each side of the tent opening. Leon Grey Squirrel stood waiting expectantly at the opposite end of the ranks.

Travis motioned Malone over to a place beside him in the line. The drums began a soft rhythm, and their leader began walking down between the two ranks, acknowledging each of their salutations.

Travis leaned and whispered in Malone's ear, "Our main man, Chief Burning Grass. Comes from beau queue generations of Miccosukee blue-bloods."

When Chief Burning Grass reached the end of the columns and stood facing Leon Grey Squirrel, he clasped arms with the medicine man in the traditional greeting, then they embraced. As the drums grew louder, Leon Grey Squirrel danced backwards around the circle, chanting, summoning the chief to follow.

The two men joined arms, the drum pace increased, and all bedlam broke loose. The men whooped and shouted and danced around and into the circle. The women trilled and danced with the children at circle's edge.

Redford, streaked back and forth through the jumble of legs, howling like a wolf. Watching in amazement as this age-old ritual played itself out, Malone relished the untainted joy exuding from man, woman, child and beast alike.

Someone tapped him on the shoulder. He turned, expecting to see Travis standing there, giving him his stupid grin.

Instead, it was Gridley James, looking like he had been on a month-long binge. His hair was stringy and heavy with oil and he had a mangy growth of beard. He smelled like a case of liverwurst waiting to explode from its own gaseous buildup.

"Hadaka say, shithead," James said, drawing a fist back.

"Not much," Malone said.

Ready this time, he deflected James's punch, then used James's off-balance, forward motion to shove him past.

James went down in a cloud of dust then scrambled quickly to his feet. He charged, flailing his arms and smashing a fist against Malone's neck and knocking him down, then jumped on top of him. James had drawn back to hit him again, when two men nearby grabbed his arms and pulled him off, struggling to contain him while another man helped Malone to his feet.

Not knowing who to bite first, Redford barked loudly, then the drums stopped and the camp grew quiet. Chief Burning Grass walked over and looked at Malone then at James.

"What's this all about? You two would dishonor our sacred traditions?"

Braves had gathered around in a tight ring of bodies. Somber-faced and speaking to each other in low voices, they pointed at the two men, disturbed by the interruption.

"Chief Burning Grass, this man is wanted by the Pinellas County sheriff," Malone said, brushing himself off. "He's a convicted felon who broke an elderly lady's arm, and raped my girlfriend after he beat both of us up."

"Yeah, and he's a nosy prick," James growled. "And a con, same as me."

Chief Burning Grass looked at each of them again. He shook his head and sighed.

"We don't live by your laws on our land. Whatever acts have been committed on the outside have no place here. We settle our differences when necessary, in traditional ways. Our ways have always proven to be just."

Chief Burning Grass conferred with Leon Grey Squirrel for a few moments, then motioned to the men holding James to bring him closer. Untying a short, braided-leather cord from his belt he looped one end around James's left wrist and cinched it tight, then looped the other end tight around Malone's left wrist, leaving them facing opposite directions with several inches of cord linking their hands.

With arms outspread, Chief Burning Grass gestured to the others to widen the circle around the two, then sat down. All the others followed suit. He motioned for silence, and when the talking had receded, he stood again and spoke in a loud voice.

"In the tradition of our warriors," Chief Burning Grass pro-claimed, clinching the cord binding the two men. "You will fight until one of you can no longer raise to his feet. If the cord comes loose or breaks, it will be retied and you will begin again. If you fall among our warriors, you will be lifted up and taken back to the center to start over. If you break bones or shed blood it is part of the ordeal, but you will not break the cord of life."

Chief Burning Grass lifted his hand then dropped it

and the drums began a slow, muffled pulsing. He nodded and lowered himself to the ground, then pulled Redford to his side and looked gravely at the pair. The men began talking among them-selves again, gesturing, quibbling over the outcome.

"I'm gonna enjoy this," James said, yanking Malone close, breathing his stench on him. "You gonna be pissin' your pants by the time I get done with you."

The one thing Malone had learned about Gridley James's methods was that he needed the element of surprise and a fair amount of distance in order to use it. Here James had neither. The Tai Kwon Do Malone had learned had taught him the basics of self-defense at close quarters. He showed James one of the easier movements before the man could blink.

Swiveling around behind him, Malone quickly hooked his right foot inside James left ankle, then swiveled again and swept his leg straight out to the front, waist high.

The upward momentum lifted James high enough for Malone to snap his leg back down while crashing his right arm across James's chest, dropping him flat on his back and knocking the wind out of him. The tether yanked Malone to a kneeling position at James's side, and the braves cheered and shouted their approval.

"We having fun yet, Gridley?" Malone said.

James lay senseless, his breath caught in his throat. For a moment, Malone wanted to smash the back of his fist upward into James's nose and drive the cartilage into his brain, ending his miserable existence.

Remembering Chief Burning Grass's warning, Malone stood quickly and planted a foot in James's armpit. Grabbing his tethered wrist with both hands, he pulled until James's arm popped out of his shoulder joint. James groaned and passed out, his disjointed arm hanging limp at the end of Malone's wrist.

The whole assembly came alive, shouting and gathering around Malone, pounding his back and ruffling his hair. Not more than three minutes had passed, and the match was over.

"Nice going, Jazz," Travis said, laughing and slapping him on the shoulder. "I knew you swabbies were good at taking out the garbage."

Chief Burning Grass pushed through the crowd and stood looking at James' dusty form and his disjointed arm hanging from Malone's wrist. With a twinkle in his eye, the Chief said the last thing in the world Malone would have expected.

"Paybacks are a bitch," he said wryly. He pulled his knife from his belt and pressed it into Malone's free hand. "Cut yourself free and tie his hands together, he's yours now. If you want to take him south, I'm sure the elders won't mind."

"I appreciate that, Chief," Malone said, severing the thong that bound him to James. "I've waited a long time for this. I'm just sorry it had to come in the middle of the festival."

Malone kneeled and rolled James up on his side. After tying his hands, he let James roll back over onto his secured arms.

Still laughing, Leon Grey Squirrel stepped out of the boisterous crowd and helped Malone to his feet. He was sniffling, wiping at his nose, and tears ran down his cheeks.

"Whoo-ee! Jasper," he said, hardly able to speak. "This is the best corn festival we've had in years! I haven't seen anybody fight like that since Steven Segal did it in a movie I seen a couple years ago."

"I wouldn't want to do that too often, it's pretty hard on the nerves," Malone said, rubbing his chaffed wrist.

"I'm curious about something, Grey Squirrel. How did this low-life happen to be here in the first place?"

Grey Squirrel shrugged. "You may not understand it, Jasper, but we allow anyone with the need to take refuge on our lands. Gridley James obviously knew that and started sniffing around one of our women, a month or so ago. Her husband's a drunk and I guess she was lonely for attention. Took this fool in and he made himself at home. Been there ever since."

"A deputy sheriff in Largo wants to see him," Malone said. "I have to figure out how to get him in the back of my truck."

"We'll take care of that," Leon Grey Squirrel said. "Travis—you and Bobby help me carry this sack of cow flop to Jasper's truck."

After paying respects all around, Malone grabbed Reddy as he zipped past, then headed for his truck. Travis, Bobby, and Grey Squirrel stood beside it grinning conspiratorially. They were proud of their rigging job.

The trio had stripped James of his clothes and tied him to the roll bars in a standing position. With arms and legs outspread, James's family jewels were in full view of any and all curious eyes.

Malone stopped at the Broken Arrow, a little bar not far from the gathering grounds. Inside the cool and sparsely decorated bungalow, he called Lt. Cobb.

"James is in slightly damaged condition, Vern," he said.

"I can be at the county line in thirty minutes." Lt. Cobb said, and hung up.

Redford was watching three very drunken Indians, standing by the tailgate and chuckling, when Malone got back to the truck. One of their even drunker friends was spitting chaws of tobacco at James, calling him every name in the book. Judging by the vitriolic nature of his words and the accuracy of his projectiles, Malone had the distinct feeling this brave might be the husband of the woman whose saddle James had been test driving.

James came to and looked around, groggy and in pain. No one present seemed to have any friendly feelings for him, but when the angry brave unsheathed an eight-inch hunting knife, then tried to climb in the back of the truck, Malone knew a trim was not what the old son had in mind.

"Hang on there, partner," he said. "He's not worth it."

Talking the four of them back inside, Malone bought a round of beers, then drank a longneck and commiserated with them. After a few quick adios's, he hopped in the truck and left.

"You prick!" James screamed over the wind. "Cut me loose, my arm's killing me! I need a drink!"

Malone responded by closing the window and giving Redford a pat. He turned the radio up louder to drown out the screams.

Malone did feel a little guilt—about leaving him that way—but he wasn't about to cut him down. Not after the evils the man had perpetrated on Anne. Left with a fresh perspective on life, Malone had had to agree with his Miccosukee friends, that in the end, nothing really mattered.

21

Lt. Cobb was waiting at the sign on Alternate U.S. Highway 19 demarcating the Pinellas and Pasco county line. Wearing a light-blue seersucker suit and his Stetson, he was puffing a cigar and drumming his fingers on the roof of the unmarked car. When Malone stopped, Cobb strolled over to look at Gridley James hanging naked from the roll bars, then slapped his knees and bent over roaring with laughter.

"Now what the hell are you up to, Jazz?" Vern whooshed. "You been making them weirdo movies or something?" He dropped the tailgate and jumped up onto the bed, then sat on the sidewall, smoking and chuckling, shaking his head in amusement.

"Nothing that exciting," Malone grinned. "Just a little karate encounter with our not-so-illustrious friend, here."

Putting on his Tampa Bay Devil Rays' cap, Malone poured Redford a bowl of water and told him to stay in the truck, then got out and went back to the tailgate and hopped up on it. His prisoner smelled worse than ever.

James struggled to free his good arm. Moaning and cursing, he only succeeded in drawing the cinches tighter. His skin had reddened in the hot sun and he flexed his pelvis, turning his knees inward, frantic to cover the bare parts department.

Lt. Cobb stood up, stepped away and peered south.

When he spoke, he turned toward James.

"Let me see here, Jazz. You know something? I'm out of my jurisdiction here. Yes sir, I'm over the county line, where we stand. I don't know…."

He pressed his dead cigar into the dirt with his toe, then sat back down beside Malone on the tailgate. His face was deadpan but his eyes were filled with glee.

"The fuck is izzat supposed to mean?" James said. "I need a doctor, Cobb. That bastard damn near ripped my arm off! And I need to get my pants on, before my…."

Lt. Cobb and Malone turned at the same time. James gazed mournfully at his penis, a rapidly darkening shade of reddish-purple in the blazing sun, despite his efforts to shade it.

"What that means, Gridley, is you can answer some questions unofficially and get some first aid within the hour," Lt. Cobb said, arching his eyebrows. "Or, you can wait for me to take you back to county jail, where we have to book you, do the paperwork, get an attorney for you. Who knows what else? Might take, what? Three, four hours, if you're lucky?"

"All right, all right, motherfucker!" James screamed, on the verge of sobbing. "Untie me, so I can put my pants on… Gee—zus, my arm hurts!"

Lt. Cobb stood up on the tailgate and fanned himself with his hat. He was enjoying this.

"You got anything we can cut him down with?" he said.

"A utility knife," Malone answered. "But you're going to have to do it. He stinks worse than a wart hog in full rut."

Malone retrieved a razor knife from his toolbox and

tossed it to Lt. Cobb. He clicked the blade out and moved at James, then wrinkled his nose and backed away, drawing his gun.

"Mind your manners, boy," Lt. Cobb growled, aiming the gun low on James's groin and sliding the safety off. "When you get your britches on, I'm going to pop that arm back in place and put the bracelets on. You can sit in the shelter of the truck for a bit. You hear me, buzzard breath?"

Handing his weapon to Malone, Lt. Cobb scrunched his face. After slowly severing the cords at each of James's wrists, he backed away.

James screamed horribly as his arm swung free, and he held it still with his good hand, the pain welling in his eyes. Grunting and cursing he managed to get his pants on, then struggled to close his jeans over tender flesh.

Malone held the gun on James as he grabbed the roll bar with his good arm. James held tight and groaned deeply as his arm went back in place with a wet click. Lt. Cobb locked the cuffs and helped him down from the truck bed.

James stumbled to the shady side of the truck and sat down, then tried to stifle his sobs. Only then did Malone feel anything for him, pity more than sympathy. Chief Burning Grass had said it right, paybacks were a bitch.

Lt. Cobb walked back to his car and returned with a six-pack of Poland Springs, lemon-flavored water he had taken from a cooler in his trunk. He gave Malone one, then uncapped a bottle and handed it to James.

"You going to Mirandize him?" Malone asked.

"Sure," Cobb said. "You have the right to...."

"Aw, don't give me that shit," James growled.

"You fucks got me right where you want me. What are rights gonna do for me?"

Leaning back against an over-sized tire, James favored his swollen arm as he drank the whole bottle in one toss. Dropping the empty, he held up cuffed hands, eyes imploring.

"Just so you know," Malone said.

"You want first crack?" Lt. Cobb said, handing Malone the remaining bottles by the plastic collar rings.

"We could do that," Malone said, trading gun for bottles. He dangled the full bottles in front of James.

"First of all, Gridley," Malone said, "what happened in the apartment that night, after you finished your little nasty with Anne on the floor?"

James grinned luridly. "You liked that, huh? She was a sweet little piece...."

Malone swung the bottles back, and Lt. Cobb grabbed his arm. "Easy does it, Jazz," he said. "He'll get his in due time. Stick to the agenda here."

Squatting in front of James, Lt. Cobb grabbed a handful of his hair. "Listen, asshole. Answer the questions or I'll pop that arm back out and leave it that way. Got it?"

James cringed and nodded. "Sadistic bastards."

Licking parched lips, he continued, "Tony shows up right when I'm bonkin' her. Screams at me to get out, go get the Hunter bitch. So, I got out."

"You weren't there when all the blood was being spilled?" Malone said, "and Tony was there while I was unconscious?"

"I don't know nothing about that shit," he said. "What I do know is before I left, I heard him yelling at Anne about some dagger, slapping her around. I was standing on the balcony trying to get my skin outta my zipper. Oh, man! Cobb? Ain't you got something for this arm?"

"Just keep talking, Gridley," Lt. Cobb said, "or I might be forced to give you an upper-body aerobics lesson."

"Did you see her leave?" Malone asked, kneeling in the shade of the truck.

"Yeah. After a few minutes she tore outta there in that green Krautmobile of hers," he said. "I went after her, but hell. The piece of shit I drive couldn't catch a fart in a paper bag."

"Who checked Mrs. Hunter in and out of the Seven Sands?" Lt. Cobb said.

"Tony and me took her up there," James said. "Tony said it was only a temporary deal."

"He had other plans, then?" Malone said.

"We got us a real Sherlock here," James snickered. "After Tony blew his stack over me doing 'his woman,' like he calls her, he gave me a signed letter. I went and got the old lady. Simple as that."

"You delivered her to the apartment?" Lt. Cobb said.

"Yup. That's the last I saw of her."

James slowly pulled his cuffed wrists back and forth across his ribcage, gently massaging his bad arm. A fly was doing touch-and-go on his face and ants had invaded his pant legs.

"Whose Caddy were you driving," Malone said, "that day on the docks when you tried to iron my shirt with me in it?"

"That's cousin J's batmobile," he said, shifting against the tire, easing his arm into a different position.

"He likes his other car better. Let's me use the Caddy when I got important movements to make."

"What kind of important movements?" Lt. Cobb said.

James did a gimme with his fingers, wiggling his tongue at the bottles of flavored water. Malone uncapped one and handed it to him and he took a long swallow, like he was sucking a cold beer, then belched and laughed.

"You guys think I'm an easy fuck or something" he said. "Twist my arm a couple times, give me some shitty stuff to drink. Gimme a break."

"What're you looking for, Gridley? Protection maybe?" Lt. Cobb said. "Got somebody to be afraid of? Somebody who might punch your ticket once you get a bed-buddy up there in Starke?"

"You got it, ace," James said. "I don't say nothing else 'til I get some kind of promises. Like a trade. Know what I mean?"

"You mean like you don't want to wake up one night," Malone said, "and discover, to your chagrin, that you're dead?"

"That's the basic idea."

"Okay, that's it, James. Let's go talk to the DA," Lt. Cobb said He leaned down like he was ready to grab James and yank him to his feet.

"Don't touch my arm!" James screamed. "You'll rip it again!" He cowered against the tire, guarding his arm, glaring. "You gotta give me something, Cobb. All you gotta do is put in a few words for me in the right places, and I'll give you a bite so big you won't be able to chew it all at once. Whaddaya say?"

Lt. Cobb gave Malone a discrete thumbs-up.

"Not saying I will and not saying I won't, James,"

Lt. Cobb said. "You better give me something worth hearing before that arm splits open and I leave you to bleed to death out here in the boonies."

James whimpered when he realized how much his arm had ballooned, holding perfectly still, like he was afraid the slightest movement would break the skin. Holding his breath, he looked from his arm to the lieutenant and back to his arm.

"Tell you what I'll do," Lt. Cobb gave James a flinty look. "You and me and Jazz will go sit in my nice, air-conditioned squad car. You tell us the good stuff while I wrap your arm in ice packs and stop the swelling. How's that sound?"

"Cobb," Malone said, "that's inside...."

"Inside a nice, cool automobile, Jazz," Lt. Cobb interrupted, shaking his head and waving Malone off. "I know I'll feel better. How about it, Gridley? You don't have to say anything more. We can sit and wait for a lawyer if you want."

Fear shadowed James's face. Staring at his arm and moaning, his eyes widened with every imagined stretch of the skin.

"What good is a lawyer gonna do me like this? I'm not gonna die am I, Cobb?" he said. "I mean, you can stop my arm from exploding, can't you?"

Lt. Cobb motioned Malone over to the front of the truck, then leaned close and spoke in a low voice.

"This one's dumber than fish bait. Let's ice him down. I'll read him his rights again, once he's loaded up and feeling secure. Just to be sure."

Helping James to his feet, they walked him to the squad car, and Malone held the back door open while James slowly lowered himself onto the seat. Lt. Cobb brought the cooler, a sheet of clear, crime-scene plastic, and a roll of duct tape around from the trunk.

Cutting and bagging the plastic loosely around James's arm, Lt. Cobb taped it along the seams and around his elbow, then scooped ice from the cooler and dumped it into the pockets he had fashioned. Packing the makeshift sling full to James's shoulder, he sealed the top edges.

Lt. Cobb got in behind the wheel and started the engine, then turned on the air-conditioning. He just finishing Mirandizing James as Malone slid in on the passenger side. Cobb hooked a finger at his computer screen: The on-board video and audio system were recording.

"Do you understand these rights as I have read them to you?" Lt. Cobb said, speaking through the security divider mesh.

"Yeah, yeah, I heard it a hundred times before," James said, mewling in relief as his arm cooled. "Don't mean jack."

"For starters, tell me what happened after you brought Mrs. Hunter back to Tony at Anne's apartment," Lt. Cobb said.

"I told you. Tony was still pissed when I got back. Yanked the old lady in the door and slammed it in my face. I left."

"Right away?"

"Like I said."

"Who is this cousin J you talked about?" Malone said.

"My old cuz, John Tanner. My momma's sister's oldest boy. Best part of him ran down his daddy's leg." James said. "He's been throwing me work for five, ten years. Doing mostly grunt stuff, like running over little bugs think they're gonna get close his action messing with his little angel daughter."

James's eyes were cold and raw.

"These important movements you mentioned," Lt. Cobb said. "Do they have anything to do with Tony?"

"That's a chuckle," James scoffed. "Tony tells me the time and place for my pickups. Crates, big nut-busters sometimes."

"In the Caddy?" Malone asked.

"With JT's warehouses and trucks? You fuck. You think I'm stupid?"

"So, Tanner knew about these pickups?" Lt. Cobb jotted notes in a small notebook he had taken from his pocket.

"Hell, yes. How you think I got the Caddy?"

"You ever see what was in the crates?" Malone asked.

Lt. Cobb nodded while he wrote, letting Malone know to keep up the line of questioning.

"I ain't gonna bust my hump and not know what was in them," James snapped. Then he got comfortable in the seat, lying down, like he was home on the couch, watching TV.

"They were sealed with plastic and had Customs' stamps. One of the big, cedar-wood bundles?" he said, smiling like he was sharing family secrets. "The plastic was split and had a couple broken boards, so I pulled one up real careful, and looked inside. Know what? It was hollowed out."

Lt. Cobb looked puzzled, then shook his head and motioned for Malone to go on.

"How come you haven't made any pickups lately?"

Malone said. "From what Chief Burning Grass said, you've been squatting with them on the reservation for a couple months."

James closed his eyes and sighed. "With jerk-offs like you nosing around, Tony told me to lay low for a while and got Harry Carson to stand in for me."

Looking sleepy, like everything was catching up to him, James mumbled, "You guys get me to a doc. My arm is nice and numb, so I'm gonna take a nap."

Lt. Cobb turned to Malone. "Come by the precinct in the next day or so. I'm going to have a chat with the assistant DA. about our friend Tony, and see if he might be interested in reopening your case."

"A glimmer of light at the end of the tunnel," Malone said

"I told you I didn't like seeing anybody getting caboosed," Vern smiled. "Get out of my squad car so I can get donkey-dung here down to lockup."

Lt. Cobb waved and pulled away.

As he sped down the highway with his lights strobing red and blue in the lengthening shadows, Malone mused on the quirkiness of the American system of justice. With prosecuting attorneys persuading judges to impose stiff bail bonds or involuntary jail time, defendants are no longer presumed innocent and permitted their freedom until they are tried and, beyond a shadow of a doubt, proven guilty. An inequitable system of justice would have its citizenry believe otherwise.

Like Shakespeare had said, Malone thought: "The first thing we do is kill all the lawyers."

22

An iridescent, cradling moon floated over Tampa
Bay as Malone cruised along North Shore Drive. A dark
portion at the north end of the beaches made a nice
pocket of star-lit privacy, for quiet interludes and
swimming in the buff.

Parking at the curb, he tuned the radio to WUSF's
jazz program. A few cars were scattered up and down the
street, so he and Redford sat in the dark, listening to a sax
man weave delightful webs, eating Whoppers and onion
rings and slurping chocolate shakes.

Malone raced Reddy across the grass and down to
the beach when they were done, stripping off his clothes
and dropping them on the sand, then following him into
the quiet waters of the bay. The dark currents ran warm
then cool, and the moon had climbed into full view across
the vastness of night, a shimmering bridal veil of pale
light and sequin stars.

They had been playing together for about twenty
minutes when a car pulled into the space next to
Frankenstein. The headlights went off, and in the
darkness a figure got out and walked down the beach to
sit at a picnic table hidden deep in the shadows, a stone's
throw from where he and Red splashed.

Reddy swam back to the shoreline and stood
quivering, his snout raised high, testing the air. He
growled then barked when the figure got up and walked

slowly toward him. Charging up the sand a few feet and stopping dead, he cocked his head, listening and sniffing, then began mewling like a puppy.

"Come here, boy," a voice called faintly over the sounds of the waves. "Come on. Don't be afraid."

Malone's pants lay on the beach and he was crouched in the water, trying not to expose his indelicate situation. He waited, not knowing quite what to do.

Redford decided it was safe and ran up to his newfound friend, licked the hand that was offered to him, then let it pet him. He danced around excited, ran back down to water's edge and barked, then ran back, yipping and gruffing. It seemed strange to Malone that Red hadn't made his usual effort to intimidate, with his growling, no-nonsense approach to strangers.

Malone's curiosity grew when their visitor began disrobing in the dim light of the moon. When all the clothes were off, the curves seemed to be in all the familiar places, and Reddy splashed in ahead of her, then swam around her as she moved closer to Malone in the water. She had her head down, her hair backlit by distant streetlights, and shielded her breasts from the cool breezes that moved across the seashore.

The moonlight glowed on her body, reflecting the lovely curve of her shoulders and hips long and sensual, and a small dark garden beckoned from the juncture of her thighs. She moved closer in the small swells, then took Malone's half-erect penis in her warm hand. The moment he touched her face, she moaned deep and low and wrapped her arms tightly around his waist.

"Oh, Jasper. I've missed you so much," she whispered, crying. "I've wanted to hold you for such a long time...."

He turned her face up and kissed her tenderly on the lips, on her cheeks, tasting her tears. Enclosing her in his arms, he breathed deep of her perfume, wanting to take her inside and keep her there forever.

"No one ever touched my heart the way you did, Anne," he said. "No matter what happened in the past, I love you and will always love you."

"I was so afraid," she said, crying softly against his chest. "After what he did to me that night, I felt so dirty and ashamed. I didn't think you would want me anymore."

"Don't talk about it right now."

"I've been past your condo a hundred times, past this beach. Hoping to see you, wanting to call."

Redford splashed happily around them as they waded to the shoreline. With ghosts from the past hovering in the trees, they dressed in silence, never taking their eyes off each other. Anne took his hand and led him over to the bench, then pulled him down next to her.

"Can I stay with you tonight?" she whispered, her head bowed and her hair veiling her face. "I'm afraid, Jazz. I don't ever want to be alone again. I need you to hold me, that's all."

Redford climbed up on the bench and lay with his head in her lap. Malone put his arm around her shoulders, and pressed his nose to her hair. As he breathed in her softness, he tried to absorb the pain she had lived with for so long, the incomprehensible fear emanating from her.

"Stay with me for as long as you need or want," he said.

Malone stood and pulled her up into his arms, holding her tightly, afraid to let go of her. Anne squeezed him, then broke away and ran to her car. When he reached the truck, he could hear her anguished crying.

Anne followed him back to the condo and parked at the curb, then rode with him into the parking garage. He opened the door of his apartment, but she waited until the lights were on before going inside. She opened the balcony door and leaned against the jamb, then wept softly as she stared at the moon.

When Malone convinced her to lie down, she took the air mattress to the balcony door and fell asleep gazing at the stars. Sitting with his back against the wall beside her, he watched her chest slowly rise and fall, and the moon had sailed beyond distant lands when he finally fell asleep, holding her hand in his.

23

Connie had taken all the furnishings out of the apartment. The intimate decorations that made it home were gone, leaving it barren and cold. The odd conglomeration of used furniture only added to Malone's sense of desolation, and became nothing more than reflectors for the hollow, echoing sounds of his footsteps.

After the first few sniffs even Redford seemed disinterested. Malone had found him at times, lying off in the corner of a bedroom, looking lost and forlorn in the emptiness.

But Anne's arrival changed all that. When Malone awoke the next morning, stiff and grouchy from sleeping on the floor, she was talking quietly on the phone. Wearing a t-shirt and a pair of his cutoffs cinched with one of his belts, she had just hung up when he stumbled into the kitchen. She poured him a cup of coffee and smiled mysteriously as he took the first few sips.

"What's up?"

"I took Reddy for a walk, earlier," Anne said. Redford was doing a slobber job on her leg.

"Good. He's acting like he enjoyed it."

"And I called the manager at my storage place and had my furniture sent here. You don't mind, do you?"

"No, of course not," Malone said, trying to shake the cobwebs loose, still a little perplexed about their meeting the night before. "You could make this place look pretty decent."

"Looks like it could stand a woman's touch," she said.

Malone poured himself a second cup of the dark brew.

"I just meant that whatever you want is fine with me"

"I have everything in storage from my apartment. Except the bedroom furniture…."

Disturbed by the memory, Anne turned her face away for a moment. Malone put his arms around her and she hugged him. Her eyes welled with tears.

"Just let it go, Anne," he said. "That's all we can do."

"Sometimes I think I'm going to have a nervous breakdown," she said. "I never went back to work for Tony. I spent entire days doing nothing but walking, on the beach or in the park, trying to sort it out."

"We'll have some dinner and wine and talk later. Right now, just relax. Everything else will follow."

"How did you get to be so wise in the ways of the world?"

"I think Connie taught me a lot more than I cared to admit," Malone said. "We did have our moments."

"You still love her, don't you?"

"Not the way I love you. Never the way I love you."

Redford was scratching at the front door, dancing around and getting antsy again. There was nothing in the refrigerator for breakfast and Malone hadn't had his third cup of coffee yet.

With Reddy on his leash, Malone and Anne walked to the Sandwich Shak on North Shore beach. Sitting on the open-air patio, they relished salt air breezes, ate bacon and egg sandwiches, and sipped hot coffee. Carried on the advancing tide, curling waves mercilessly washed away a huge sandcastle a sun-bronzed old man wearing a red beret and a blue bikini had built on the packed sands near the end of a sandbar.

* * *

That afternoon, with Redford huddling in the Porsche's utility space, Malone drove Anne to the Shady Oaks mobile home park in Seminole where she had taken refuge after that fateful day. She packed her clothes in two large suitcases and left the key at the park manager's office, saying she wouldn't be back, but she would call. She kissed and hugged the bespectacled, elderly woman like she was saying goodbye to her grandmother.

While Malone went into the Kash N' Karry supermarket for groceries, Anne sat in the car with Reddy, singing along with a Chris Rea tune on the radio. When he came out, she had opened the T-top, and was playing with the boy's ears, kissing him and laughing each time he licked her face.

Malone put steaks on the hibachi and Anne uncorked a bottle of Cabernet Sauvignon Beringer, then they sat on the balcony savoring each bite and every sip and making small talk. The sun nestled down into pink, billowing clouds and the lights of downtown St. Petersburg sparkled in the dusk, like fairies flitting among mountain caves, searching for mislaid treasures.

The wine and the views had their effects. Anne was more relaxed and sat close to Malone, her hair rippling like silk in the breeze and her soft eyes mirroring the skyline. He meditated on the tinkling sound of a small wind chime off in the distance, being danced about by a puckish zephyr.

"Did you know Tony had a key to my place?" she said, her eyes dark and mysterious.

"I suspected he did," Malone said, remembering Tony's revelation at the lake. "Didn't he give it back to you after you broke it off with him?"

Anne bit at her lip and pulled the hair away from her eyes.

"He wouldn't give it to me. When I phoned, he said if I wanted it bad enough I would to come to him."

"What did your folks say about that?"

"My father actually laughed. He said Tony could make me a rich woman."

"What about your mother?"

"She was silent about the whole thing. She believed from the start Tony was the best thing that ever happened to me."

Anne stood up and leaned against the balcony railing.

"It sounds like they expected you to marry him."

"Tony did too. When I broke-up with him, he threatened me. He said I would never be with anyone else, not while he was alive. He would see to it."

Anne's face was hidden in the shadows, her voice trembling as she struggled to express her anger and grief. Malone held many of the same feelings about that night but knew one memory was etched in stone for her.

"Anne. I have to ask you something. You don't have to answer me…," Malone said, standing and gently massaging her shoulders. "Do you know anything about your father's business?"

She sighed then leaned back against him, releasing her self to the warm strength of his hands. If she had any reluctance for talking about her father, it was not apparent in her answer.

"Not the particulars. I do know that he and Tony were always having meetings about my father's various holdings. Tony and I often had to cancel our plans. When my father called, Tony answered no matter when or where," she said, bitterly. "I hated my father and eventually Tony because of that."

"What did Tony want from you that night?" Malone said.

Anne stiffened for a moment and trembled.

"Somehow, he found out that before Mrs. Hunter started having memory loss, she had sent the dagger to him."

"Why did he get angry with you?"

"Because she had mailed the package," Anne said. "The day it was delivered no one was in the office to accept it, so they left a delivery notice stuck on the door."

Malone poured the last of the wine and sat down, hoping her willingness to talk would continue. Standing alone at the railing she was lost in thought and had begun to shiver.

"Can we go inside?" Anne said, opening the balcony door. "I'm getting a chill."

She sat on the air mattress next to the coffee table with her legs crossed, and the baggy cut-offs made her look fragile and innocent. Redford laid down beside her and flopped his head in her lap. She stroked his neck, putting him in a trance, then after a few minutes he was sound asleep.

Malone sat next to her on the mattress and sipped

his wine.

"So, can I assume that Tony if not in actual possession of the dagger has had the delivery notice all along?"

Anne shook her head then sipped from her glass. There was an indefinable sadness in her face when she looked at him.

"I had the notice in my purse and after work the next day I picked up the package. Part of my job is to open Tony's mail and packages, most of which are usually legal documents. I simply forgot about it—the dagger—and put it with my collection at my apartment. I intended to give it to him."

"But he found the dagger at your place before you had a chance to give it to him."

"He had it in his hand that night," Anne said. "He looked... fanatical, like he was ready to...."

"...To use it on you?" Malone said quietly.

Head down, Anne nodded.

"Did you know it was contraband? Your father smuggled it into the country by switching it with another knife."

"No, I didn't know," Anne said. "I knew something was going on, though. I visited my mother one evening while he was in a meeting with Tony and two Latino men. One of them was my father's shipping agent, Julio Ramirez, and the other one I didn't recognize. Tony was screaming at them, about messing up a shipment aboard a vessel called the Vista Azure."

Anne was tense, the references to Tony awakening dragons. It seemed Tony had become more volatile with each passing day and Anne had born the brunt of his obsessive raging.

"Why don't we try this again tomorrow? Malone said.

Her revelations had sapped away any feelings of intimacy. He would not sleep but he would be comforted knowing a little more of her wall had crumbled away.

While Anne showered, he made up a bed for her, then heard her talking to Reddy as he sat by the window. Lost beneath the spangled canopy of night, he ruminated on how men like Tony could be so cruel to the people they supposedly loved one day, then look at themselves in the mirror the next.

Apparently, John Tanner's operations and security had a higher priority with Tony than any possible damage he might inflict on others. Malone thought of Tina Turner's singing "What's love got to do with it?"

In the morning he gave Anne a set of keys, then stopped at the condo office and told Mrs. Anderson he needed the elevators set-up for Anne's furniture. After a typical dressing-down from her about changing the occupancy agreement, Malone drove to Largo and the Pinellas County sheriff's offices.

Lt. Cobb was sitting on the front steps in short sleeves, with his tie tucked into his shirt and his holster and badge clipped to his belt. He had peeled an orange and tossed the skins in the flowerbed, and was spitting the seeds at one of the planters standing beside the front doors. His chin was dripping with juice, and he launched another seed at the planter when Malone walked up. Cobb looked upset.

"You know what that clown McFarland went and did? He got wind of my bringing Gridley James in, so he got a federal prosecutor to order my department to produce a body. I can understand them wanting to move on John Tanner, but where in hell am I going to find a body?"

Malone leaned against the portico abutment and Cobb reached into a brown paper bag, pulled out two pink guavas and handed him one. A squad car came screaming out of the compound, its lights and siren going, and smoked the tires down Ulmerton Road.

"I keep telling those guys…," he said, shaking his head. "One of these days they're going to sideswipe somebody or something worse. I hate to even think about the worse part."

Malone took small bites of the guava, relishing the tart flavor of the meat and remembering the days when he, Vern, and Tony used to roam the neighbor-hood on their bicycles looking for ripening guavas. How they would park the little gems on their windowsills and wait for the moment of perfect ripeness.

"Do you remember any of the particulars the morning I was arrested at the lake?" Malone said.

"Yeah, I remember," Lt. Cobb said. "We found you covered in blood, looking like some wild creature that had just finished gorging on the wet insides of a deer carcass."

"That's not what I mean. Did you take note of who else was there when you arrived on the scene?"

"Well, let's see. There was you and your truck and the four officers and their squad cars," Lt. Cobb said, finishing his guava, crunching the seeds and all. "Oh, yeah. Tony was there. Is that everybody?"

"Did you know Tony was already there when I pulled in?"

Lt. Cobb squinted at him questioningly, pulled out his handkerchief and unfolded it slowly. After wiping his hands, he neatly refolded it and tucked it back into his hip pocket.

"You told me that. And I told you, that's not what Tony said. He said when he drove up, you were disposing of the evidence—same way his statement read. What did you call it?"

"Adminicular evidence," Malone said, tossing the guava core in the flowerbed on top of Vern's peelings. "He lied that day, and in his statement. I may have been a little out of it, but it looked to me like he may have been there for quite a while. He was just polishing off a pint of whiskey when I drove up."

"He did look a little wild-eyed," Lt. Cobb said. "At the time I wrote it off to his partying or something."

"He was partying all right. Just not in any normal way like you or I would."

Lt. Cobb moved over and sat on the abutment across from Malone as two young women led a ragged, noisy column of well-dressed, four- and five-year-old kids up the steps and into the station. He saluted back when a tousle-haired boy raised a small hand to his forehead. The boy giggled, wide-eyed, to his pal.

When they were all inside, Malone took the lieutenant's place on the steps. The sun was beginning to heat the air.

"Remember what James said about Tony being in the apartment that night?" he said.

Lt. Cobb took a cellophane-wrapped toothpick from his shirt pocket and unwrapped it. Sheer joy filled his face as he picked the grit of the guava seeds from between his teeth.

"Something about his being angry. Can't say as I blame him. I walk in on a rape, somebody's going to get their privates stitched to their upper lip."

"That wasn't what he was mad about."

"How do you know that? James said Tony walked in on him while he was doing Anne. I'd say that was reason enough, wouldn't you?"

"Last night Anne told me it was because she had the dagger," Malone said. "She also said Tony looked like he was ready to use it on her."

"Wait a minute, Roscoe. You saying Anne and the dagger are now somewhere in our fine locale?

"Come on, Vern. After being raped by a felon, then assaulted by an old boyfriend, who just happens to be your father's attorney—what would you do?"

Lt. Cobb was boiling over. He took his gun out of the holster, eying it and hefting it in one hand, then tossing it back and forth from one hand to the other.

"If I wasn't such a stable-minded person," he growled, slipping the gun back into its holster and snapping it down, "I think I'd want to blow somebody's freaking head off."

He stood up and brushed the seat of his pants off, then crooked a finger at Malone and said, "Let me get my coat, then let's you and me take a ride over to McFarland's office in Tampa. I have a feeling he'll want to talk to you about Mr. Amato, and I know he'll want to speak with Ms. Hurt, now she's back in circulation."

When they rolled into Tampa, Lt. Cobb went ahead to McFarland's office while Malone stopped in the lobby of the federal building to call Anne. The Veteran's Affairs offices were just around the corner, and a motley group of veterans was staging a sit-in, waving banners and pounding drums, chanting about President Bush's plans to reduce their benefits. Various television reporters, their lights raising the ambient temperature a couple of sweltering notches, shouted and scrambled for position, making it nearly impossible for Malone to hear what Anne was saying.

She yelled that the movers had arrived but were having trouble getting her one of her sofa sections in the elevator. She said she would lock-up when they were done, and would be over as soon as possible.

Malone repeated his cell phone number to her and hung up. Walking to the elevators he saw Travis Raintree, sitting in the front row pow-wow fashion. He was berating a bewildered looking, bald-headed man wearing a V.A. nametag who happened to be standing at the front of the protest group. Travis spotted him, waved, then went back to his tirade.

Striding into the FBI offices, Malone thought he had mistakenly turned the wrong way: modern, executive style furnishings, plush carpet, coordinated prints on walls, and the hushed aura of an institutional think-tank. If staff members were present, they were squirreled away and working quietly.

"Can I help you?" a young, well-dressed man asked. The kid couldn't have been more than twenty-two or three, Malone thought, probably right out of college and into the fire.

"I'm looking for Special Agent McFarland."

"Down the hall, third door on the right."

Malone found the conference room and walked in. Special Agent McFarland was sitting at the end of a long, solid oak table and had nearly a quarter of the table's surface covered with folders, pictures, and agency reports. McFarland and Lt. Cobb were arguing, but stopped the moment he appeared.

"Where's Miss Hurt?" McFarland barked, looking at his watch. "We can't start until she gets here. Not to mention I have to draft a preliminary report for the assistant director and have it on his desk by five today."

"She'll be here, Agent McFarland," Malone said, slipping into the chair next to Cobb. "Not everyone snaps to attention when the boss farts, you know."

McFarland turned red above the collar, and sat gritting his teeth. He began shuffling through some papers and clicking his ballpoint pen like he was sending Morse code. Cobb was trying hard not to laugh.

"I guess we could start without her," McFarland said. "At least your version of the events, anyway."

Cobb picked up a page from a folder he had laying open in front of him and handed it to Malone.

"I think the best place to start is with the statement Tony gave me at the lake," he said.

Malone was puzzled by Tony's verbal accountings about the way he claimed things transpired.

"He swore I was already at the lake when he got there," he said. "In actuality it was the other way around—he got there first. Gridley James can attest to the fact that the night of the murder, the night before my arrest, while I was unconscious, Tony was at the apartment for quite a while. But he wasn't there when I came to."

"We can't give much credence to what Mr. James has to say," McFarland said. "Not when his claim to fame includes an alleged rape, documented strong-arm tactics, and now, accessory to drug-smuggling and organized crime."

"What do you mean alleged, McFarland?" Malone said. "I was there."

"Regardless of what you think of Gridley James, Mac," Lt. Cobb said, "we still have Anne Hurt to corroborate most of what Jazz is saying."

"Tony was acting bizarre when I talked to him that morning by the lake," Malone said. "He kept looking at the blood on my clothes, then wide-eyed at his own hands, holding them out like there was something on them, something he didn't want to get on his clothes. The whole scene was very strange."

"Seems out of character for Tony," Cobb added. "He was in a big hurry to get away from there, I remember. My immediate thought was, with all his legal training, he'd stick around, his being a witness and all."

McFarland grunted as he shuffled through one of the folders. Finding what he wanted, he spun a photo down the table to Malone.

"That the car he was driving, at the lake?"

Malone looked at the color glossy one of their agents had snapped of Tony emerging from his Mercedes. Looking directly at the camera and smiling, like it was a publicity pose.

"That's it," he said, handing the photo to Cobb.

McFarland slid another photo down. "Is this Esther Hunter?"

Malone looked at it momentarily, and then passed it on.

"She's a lot older than that now, but, yeah, that's her."

There was a knock on the door, and Anne walked in. Behind her was the upright citizen himself, John Tanner. The older man following them was Charles Brannon, senior member of Tony's law firm. Carrying a briefcase and looking disgruntled, the nattily dressed

Brannon was just closing his cell phone.

24

In the annuls of ancient mythology it is recorded that when the Greeks mounted attacks against the walls of Troy they used the classical approach, bringing the brute strength of their armies to bear against the Trojan embattlements. The Grecian command soon realized their efforts were being wasted, and employed an element of surprise never before used.

Playing off the renowned pride of their enemy, the Greeks placed a victor's trophy outside the Trojan gates: a massive, wooden horse. Accepting it as a sign of their victory, the Trojans wheeled it inside the city walls. As the author wrote, the Greeks emerged from hiding during the night and sprung an unexpected, highly successful attack from within the heart of the city. Thus the infamous wooden horse, and with minimal effort the Greeks conquered the Trojans and won the war.

John Tanner had no subterfuge as clever as a wooden horse, but his surprise attack--from within his enemy's own camp--was just as bewilderingly potent. If respected for nothing else, he deserved accolades for his ingenious methods. He had caught his opponents off guard and had accomplished it with an uncommon dignity and flair.

McFarland slid photos under papers, closed and stacked file folders, then turned as many pages face down as he could without seeming obvious. He rose, adjusted his suit and tie, then sat back down, looking like he had been caught participating in some questionable activity in a public restroom.

Lt. Cobb walked around the table to pull a chair out for Anne. When they were all seated, he sat next to Malone.

Malone thought the whole charade was interesting, since McFarland didn't know which way to look. He was enchanted by the fact that, with Tanner, Anne, and the attorney on one side, and Vern and him on the other, McFarland looked confused about which side of the line of battle he should be on, sitting with two opposing generals looking over his shoulders.

Tanner quietly conferred with his attorney. After waving the lawyer off, he looked with interest at McFarland.

"I am advised to state I'm here under my own free will," he said in a soft, well-modulated voice. "To protect my wife's and daughter's interests in this affair, and propose a resolution to our mutual problem."

McFarland shook his head. "We can discuss our options, Mr. Tanner, but that's all. What did you have in mind?"

A smile tugged at the corner of Tanner's mouth. If ever molds were cast of famous poker faces, Tanner's would be displayed among the best. Brown eyes distorted behind thick, rose-tinted glasses. He had salt and pepper hair, perfectly combed back on his head. A smooth face, showing not a wrinkle or line of stress: the inscrutable image of a rich businessman.

"It will be substantiated by way of sworn testimony that neither Mr. Tanner's daughter nor his wife had knowledge of his business dealings," Brannon said.

"What do you have to offer?" Lt. Cobb said. "We already have enough to charge them as accessories."

"I doubt that," Brannon said, "We will prove…."

Tanner touched Brannon's sleeve, stopping him in mid-sentence. It was clear with whom the power lay.

"Tony Amato," Anne said.

"All well and good, Ms. Hurt," McFarland said, clicking his pen. "But we need more than that to consider any agreements."

"What Anne is implying, Agent McFarland," Malone said, "is that Mr. Tanner may be able to produce specific details about Tony's involvement in my case."

"Care to expound on that, Mr. Tanner?" McFarland said.

Tanner nodded at Malone, then directed his attention back to McFarland.

"We will require a signed affidavit from your director, stating my family will not be involved in this," Tanner said.

McFarland sat back, seemingly relaxed, contemplating Tanner's demand. His pen clicking reached a frantic pace.

"I don't have the authority to make that kind of agreement. You'd have to take that up with the federal prosecutor."

"Well, I do have the authority, Mac," Lt. Cobb said, slamming his hand down on the table. Malone could almost see fire and smoke pouring from his nostrils.

"Until I produce a body this murder investigation still falls under local jurisdiction," he said. "Mr. Tanner. Unless I tell you otherwise you'll have your affidavit—and the Sheriff's backing on it."

"Thank-you, Lt. Cobb, Tanner intoned. "It's nice to

know the Pinellas County sheriff's office still has some feelings for one of its major benefactors and supporters."

Lt. Cobb scowled. "Don't get chummy with me, Tanner. We know all about your sources, so get on with it."

Charles Brannon looked as if Lt. Cobb had just announced the end of the world. Malone considered the absurdity of the assumptions men like Brannon and Tanner made, that wealth brings with it unlimited freedom and power.

"I was only trying to be polite, lieutenant," Tanner said.

"I'm advising against this, Mr. Tanner," Brannon stated. "With regard to any pending federal charges, that is."

"It's all right, Charles," Tanner said, "I think I can trust these gentlemen to handle this appropriately.

Brannon remained silent but frustration lined his face. The elderly attorney wasn't accustomed to having his advice so capriciously ignored.

"I'm willing to make a sworn statement," Tanner went on, "concerning Mr. Amato's role in facilitating the death of Mrs. Esther Hunter, also known as Aunty Q, I believe."

McFarland stood up abruptly and stepped to the telephone resting on a rose-colored credenza behind his chair. He punched in a number and turned to Tanner. "Mind if we record your statement, Mr. Tanner?"

"You've been recording my conversations and my movements for quite some time now, Agent McFarland," Tanner said, breaking into a smile. "Without my permission, I might add. Why would I object now?"

Looking nonplussed, McFarland spoke into the

phone. A few minutes later a young woman with short black hair and a business suit came in and sat down. She laid out a writing pad, a micro cassette recorder and several spare tapes. Turning the recorder on, she spoke the date, time, and the names of everyone present, then told McFarland she was ready.

McFarland told everyone to stand and take an oath. Beads of sweat glistened on his upper lip as he swore them in.

"Please proceed, Mr. Tanner," he said, sitting down. He prepared to make notes on a yellow legal pad.

Lt. Cobb produced his notebook and a Swisher Sweet, jammed the tipped cigar in his mouth and started scribbling. His expression was that of a schoolboy who's just been told to write on the blackboard one hundred times, 'I will not make promises to drug dealers.'

"Tony called me late one night," Tanner said. "I can assume from what Anne has told me that it was the night before Mr. Malone was arrested. He seemed very agitated and said he had recovered the dagger. When I questioned him as to which dagger he was referring to, he said I knew exactly which dagger."

Tanner paused, looking around with the hint of a sneer on his face, saying he knew they knew about the illegitimacy of the dagger but not admitting outright ownership.

"When I told him to get to the point he said, and I quote, 'I have permanently taken care of the problems we've been having with your daughter and old lady Hunter.' Not having the slightest idea of what he was talking about, I asked him what he meant by that, what problem?"

Tanner stopped, reached across and poured himself

a glass of water from the decanter sitting at the middle of the table. He drank slowly until the entire glass was empty, then refilled it and sat it on the table in front of him.

"He seemed very angry," he continued, "and started yelling something about Anne being...excuse me, ladies...a whoring bitch, and that she would burn in hell for her betrayal of him. When I asked him what he meant by that, he said he had let himself into Anne's apartment, had walked in on her and, in his words, 'she was doing it on the floor with that animal, James, right after she had done it with Malone.'"

Anne had her head down, crying softly. Tanner pulled out a handkerchief and offered it to her, then put his hand on her shoulder and whispered to her. She pulled away from him, then took a tissue from her clutch and touched it to the corners of her eyes.

"What does this have to do with the alleged murder of Mrs. Hunter?" Lt. Cobb said. "Just because Tony saw Gridley James...,"

Glancing at Anne, Cobb stopped short of saying it, but went on. "His seeing James engaged in an illegal sex act and his knowing about Jazz and Anne's obvious physical relationship doesn't prove he's a murderer."

"May I say something?" Anne said, pulling her hair away from her face she looked at Cobb. "You wouldn't believe how obsessive Tony was, Lt. Cobb. One night when we went out together, he came very close to beating a man senseless just for buying me a drink. Before I ran out of the apartment that night, he threatened me with the dagger. He was...slapping me, waving it in my face, acting...psychotic. Almost like he wanted to use it on me. If I hadn't managed to get at least a coat on while he was in that incoherent state and ran out, I'm certain now he would have used it on me."

Lt. Cobb leaned over and whispered to Malone, "That's basically what James told us about Tony the other day…."

Tanner patted Anne on the shoulder and she gave him a menacing look. He pulled away, then folded both hands on the table. She got up, then walked around the long end of the table and sat down next to Malone. The ultimate rejection from his only child, and Tanner had paid dearly for it.

"Continue, Mr. Tanner," McFarland said, chewing on his fingernail like he hadn't eaten in three days, the pen clicking interrupted only by the occasional notation on his pad.

Before Tanner could respond, McFarland said, "What I would like to know is—Mr. Tanner—how you think giving us Tony Amato equates to any form of protection for your family?"

"Because, Agent McFarland," Charles Brannon interrupted. "Mr. Tanner knows where the body is, and Anne knows where to find the dagger in question." Turning, he went on. "With that kind of concrete evidence, Lt. Cobb, could you not, through evidentiary procedures, demonstrate it was Tony who committed the crime? And would that not be sufficient evidence to shield Mr. Tanner's family from this despicable and morbid affair?"

Despite all that Brannon had said, at the mention of the most obviously missing part of his investigation, Lt. Cobb's face brightened. "That would depend on my department's crime lab taking possession of the body and the dagger."

"I can tell you where they are, lieutenant," Tanner said. "But I find the idea of being subjected to the sight of a mutilated, desiccating corpse extremely distasteful. I would prefer not to go there."

"You're not in any position to bargain on this one, Tanner." Lt. Cobb stewed. "I can charge you with being an accessory after, so how about you just tell me and I'll decide who goes where and does what."

Anne gripped Malone's arm, then leaned forward. "Tony put the dagger back in my collection that night, lieutenant. I didn't realize that until I unpacked all my personal things. Without thinking, I hung it in the display case with all my other knives at Jazz's condo."

"Oh, for crying out loud!" Cobb raged. "How am I supposed to explain to the DA that I have a murder weapon, a contraband dagger, handled by umpteen grubby hands hanging in a display in the condo of the original murder suspect?"

"I can arrange to have our lab can do an electron-microscope analysis on the dagger," McFarland offered. "Might find partials, maybe even traces of Mrs. Hunter's blood. That would be predicated on allowing federal assistance with your investigation, Lt. Cobb."

"Deal," Lt. Cobb said, trying hard not to look pleased. "That only leaves the body, Mr. Tanner."

Tanner leaned back in his chair and crossed his arms and legs. Outwardly distressed, he studied Cobb, trying by some psychic means to burn the notion of his having to go along out of Cobb's head.

"I'll call Bill Wilson, he said, finally. "He's SWEFAP manager at my cold storage facility in Oldsmar."

Lt. Cobb blanched. "Cold storage? You mean to tell

me Mrs. Hunter's body has been on ice for the past two years?"

"In quick frozen vegetables," Tanner nodded, "locker B-12, Wilson told me. Last row, bottom shelf. Wilson was there the night Tony brought…it in."

"Did Wilson know what was in the package?" McFarland asked.

"I doubt it. Tony probably told him it was butchered alligator he wanted to store, for use at a later date. By law, Wilson is required to have unknown food products inspected for contamination. When he reported it to me, I told him to keep quiet, I would handle it myself."

"Did Wilson say whether or not Tony was driving his Mercedes when all this took place?" Malone asked.

"No, he didn't. But I think you could safely assume he was," Tanner said. "He never drove anything else that I'm aware of. Wouldn't consider it, despite the nature of his obligations to me. I told him several times his conspicuous displays would catch up to him and obviously they did."

"But not the way you were expecting," McFarland added.

"That's enough about that, Mr. Tanner," Brannon interjected. "We'll need to review any further evidence before we issue a formal statement."

Tanner held both hands out, palms up, and shrugged.

Eyebrows raised; Lt. Cobb glowed like a beauty queen. "Hot damn! Means we can warrant a sweep of his car and likely find enough to lock and load."

"Are we through here?" Tanner said. "Mr. Brannon is right. I have nothing else to offer right now and I have matters to attend to before I turn myself in."

Consternated, McFarland stood up. "Mr. Tanner. In my official capacity as an agent of the Federal Bureau of Investigation of the United States," he said hurriedly, "I am remanding you to the authority of Lt. Vernon Cobb, deputy of the Pinellas County sheriff, until further action by our agency is taken. If you attempt to leave this jurisdiction, you will be arrested by federal marshals and you will be incarcerated until such time as your case can be adjudicated. Do you understand my instructions?"

"Yes, I do," Tanner replied. "I will fully comply under guidance of legal counsel. Exclusive of Mr. Amato, of course."

"Thanks for your assistance, Agent Collins," McFarland said, with a quick slice across his neck. "I'll get with you later on the transcripts."

Tanner stood and made a move for the door. Charles Brannon snapped his briefcase closed and moved quickly to follow.

"You just hang on there, Tanner," Lt. Cobb said loudly. "I got a couple calls to make. Then we're gonna to take a ride out to your vegetable morgue and take a gander at something that's not featured in any restaurant."

It was Tanner's turn to blanch. He may have been a restaurant owner, but it was clear from his reaction he never really knew what went on in the kitchen.

Cobb turned to Anne and Malone with a big grin. "Why don't you two go home and have some— whatchamacallit—rest? I'll send a deputy by to pick up the dagger. Don't you dare touch it, Malone. You would be back up the proverbial creek."

"Let me know about Tony, would you?" Malone said.

"You want to be there when we take him down?"

"Not necessarily, Vern. You, Tony, and I go back a long way. I can empathize for what he's about to go through."

"The old locomotive effect, eh?"

"Yeah."

Anne raised on her toes and kissed Cobb on the cheek, then shot her father a scathing look.

Both were quiet in the truck on the way back. When Malone unlocked the door of the condo, Anne wrapped her arms around his neck and gave him a wet kiss, wiggling her groin against him. Laughing, she pulled away and swept the door open.

It was beautiful; Anne had arranged everything nearly the same way as her apartment. The long, sweeping sectional was against the wall; prints and photographs were hung in their places; and her bamboo-screened collection of knives divided the dining area from the living room.

Anne took Malone by the hand and led him around to the knife display. She was quiet as her eyes scanned for the dagger. Then she stepped closer and examined the black-jade artifact. She was breathing in shallow stops and starts, almost unable to restrain her trembling hand from picking it up.

"Isn't it spooky?" she said. "I mean, just knowing someone was murdered with it. It's awful."

"That's what the Mayans used it for" Malone said. "They didn't consider it murder though. It was religious sacrifice, an age-old and honorable tradition."

Anne's eyes had an unfathomable light to them. Hypnotic, they seemed able to penetrate to Malone's soul.

"You know something?" she said. "The first time I handled it I felt something coursing up my hands and arms, like it was…magical. No, orgasmic almost. I don't remember putting it down. Isn't that strange?"

Something stirred in Malone's memory, something vaguely disturbing. His trips to Guatemala had given him a new respect for the ancients. Crime was probably a virtual unknown in a society that sacrificed their teenagers and traditionally rewarded their best sports teams with death.

"Legend has it that Mayan priests used it to cut their sacrificial victim's heart out," he said. "Strange custom. Spend the early years of your life being treated like royalty. The best foods, the best clothing, every wish fulfilled. Then you reach your late teens or early twenties and some priest comes along and says it's your turn to kiss the dagger."

"I couldn't handle that," Anne said. "I'd take my own life if I knew some guy was going to cut my heart out immediately after the big party."

"At the Chitzen Itza compound, deep in the jungles of the Yucatan Peninsula in Mexico, there's a huge pit, an almost perfect circular hole in the ground near the Temple of the Warriors. If you didn't like the dagger routine, you could, with royal splendor, throw yourself off a sacred platform and fall nearly a hundred feet to your drowning death."

Anne gave him an ominous look.

Redford tip-toed out of the bedroom and sneaked up behind Malone, then with a loud snort, goosed him. He jumped, Anne jumped, and both collapsed to the carpet laughing. Reddy climbed over them, licking and drooling exuberantly.

Anne unzipped Malone as he boxed with Reddy, her hands tentatively exploring long-lost territories. He could do nothing except lie back and enjoy the sensations she was producing in his long-neglected body.

The telephone warbled and Malone considered letting it go: Anne had resurrected a phenomenon he hadn't experienced in a while. He waddled to the phone gripping his drooping pants.

"Malone and Associates, and this really better be good."

"Jasper?" Lt. Cobb said. "Listen. You and Anne get your tails down here right now. We got a problem."

"Where is here, Vern?" Malone said. "and I'm really busy at the moment. What's so important it can't wait?"

"I'm at the Compton office building," Cobb said. "Tampa police's SWAT team just went up to the thirty-eighth floor. Take a shot at the problem?"

"Sure. Tony's holed-up in his office and is going to kill himself or somebody else if he doesn't get something he wants?"

"Malone, you watch too much TV.," Vern said. "He's holed-up in his office all right, and has a gun. Says he won't give himself up until he's had a chance to talk to you. I think Anne should be there, too."

"It's not going to happen that way. I'll try to talk with him, but I won't jeopardize Anne in the process."

"Let her decide, Jazz," he said. "She might have better luck talking him out and we could avoid a nasty scene."

"All right," Malone said. "We'll be there."

He regretted saying it the moment he hung-up.

25

Lit by swaths of rainbow-hued laser lighting, Compton Towers were an architecturally stunning sight among lesser constructs. Crenellated columns, tall arching window casements, fountains tiled in Spanish mosaics. The owner's vision was completed with muted-pink brick landings spiraling gently toward a beveled-glass enclosed lobby. Causal events were marring that vision though, unfolding at a demonic pace, and the evening would take an unimaginable turn.

Thrill seekers were spilling onto Franklin Street when Anne and Malone arrived. Great wallowing trucks porcupined with satellite dishes and antennas had settled in. Television crews jousted with cameras and lighting fixtures, and miles of cabling set the stage for the perfect street-side interviews, to be broad-cast live with full details at eleven.

Tampa police were cordoning off side streets leading to the towers with marked and unmarked cruisers. A small army of officers jostled with hordes of reporters trying to penetrate the barricades and run into the building for the first scoop on what was rapidly turning into a media-driven circus.

"We're out front, Vern," Malone said, when he answered his cell phone.

"I'll be down in a few minutes. You're cleared, but you have to wear vests, so be prepared. It's a madhouse up here—one like you've never seen."

Lt. Cobb's description fell short of reality. On the thirty-eighth floor, SWAT officers wearing headsets and combat gear and holding automatic weapons looking hyped and abrasive as they guarded every hall-way and door.

Communications specialists were nervously wiring into the telephone lines, while a shaved-head, testosterone-charged tactical coordinator, garbed in a black, quasi-military uniform, shouted commands at them and over his radio.

Wearing heavy Kevlar vests, Anne and Malone were accosted by police officers at every turn and Redford yanked at his leash, his ears laid back aggressively. Even in full deputy's uniform, Lt. Cobb struggled to get them safely through the mayhem of the carpeted hallway to the law offices.

The waiting room of Baxter, Brannon, Moss and Amato had been turned into a command post, an un-settling and unceasing maelstrom of activity. Numerous plain-clothes detectives with badges hung around their necks stood talking at Ellen McVee's desk, which had been cleared of all its accouterments. Crowded with three telephones, a complex transceiver set, two monitors, a speaker and a running VCR, helter-skelter cabling ran in every conceivable direction.

The desk was manned by a sole, crew-cut young man wearing a light blue jogging suit and running shoes. He looked harried as he simultaneously talked on the phone, scanned the monitors, and flipped through various officious-looking notebooks.

"Here's the situation," Lt. Cobb said. "We've had Tony on the phone long enough to determine he's got a female hostage. One of the paralegals—name's Carol Martin. Tactical teams have the rear corridor leading to his office secured and they've inserted a camera probe for a visual on the room."

Lt. Cobb pointed at the monitors: a small, oval-shaped image of the office showing Tony at his desk appeared on one of the screens. He looked drunk, waving the gun like a wild man, slapping Carol Martin around.

A plain-clothes detective stepped over and tapped Cobb on the shoulder. He was grim-faced and reticent and wiped a hand over his face before he spoke.

"We got him on the line, Cobb. It's crazy in there."

"Jazz, this is Detective Smits," Lt. Cobb said. "He's Task Force C.O., and in charge. This is Jasper Malone, detective, and Anne Hurt, his fiancée."

Smooth-skinned and thin, with wavy black hair and high Euro-Spanish features, Detective Smits gave Anne the once over as he gripped Malone's hand, then started when he saw Reddy. He reached down to pet him and Reddy growled. Smits pulled back like he had been bitten.

"No offense, detective," Malone said. "Redford's pretty nervous right now."

"None taken, Mr. Malone. We're all a little tight, considering the circumstances," Detective Smits said. "What's your game plan, Cobb? I'm coming up short on this one."

"For starters, let's get Jazz on the phone with him," Cobb said. "See if he can make sense of Tony's ramblings."

Detective Smits grunted and hooked a finger at Malone, then waded to the communications table and handed him a headset patched into a routing box and the external speaker. Coming from the speaker were the rising and falling sounds of Tony's diatribe, as he expiated whatever was eating at his soul.

"Talk to him, Jazz," Detective Smits said. "Get a feel for what's going on in his head. Get him distracted so our shooters can get closer."

"No! Please," Anne said. The blood had drained from her face and she was hugging herself. "Isn't there another way?"

A woman's ragged screams could be heard intermittently in the background. A voracious and deadly ritual, born of a desperate mind, was about to begin.

"I can't do this," Malone said.

"Talk about college or the old days in the neighborhood, Jazz," Vern said. "Just get him settled down so we can work with him."

Tony had suddenly stopped his jabbering. No sounds came from the speaker or headset.

"Tony?" Malone said softly. "It's Jasper, Tony. Are you there?" He heard breathing, then Tony spoke in a guttural voice.

"What're you doing here, asshole?" he rasped drunkenly. "Come to see my grand finale? Me and little Carol-ee are having a party. Want to join us? I feel shitty. Must have drank too much of the old Jim Bomber."

"Vern's here with me, Tony. We were wondering if we could come in and have a drink, celebrate old times with you."

"It'd be nice, Jazz, but I think I'm out of booze. Let me check and see...."

The receiver clunked down, and watched and listened as Tony stumbled around in the background. He was mumbling, opening drawers, then something crashed to the floor.

"Son-of-a-bitch. Lamp cost me a bundle. She got what was coming, ripping JT off like that." Tony fumbled the phone, then breathed hard into the receiver.

"We're on, Jazz," he said, "but just you, not Marshall Dillon. You and I got a certain matter to discuss. And bring Donna Preston with you, I want some airtime."

Detective Smits was shaking his head, motioning Malone to cut it off. A private meeting was not part of his strategy.

"I'll be there in a few minutes, Tony," Malone said. "Redford's here, bud. Can he come in?"

"Bring the old boy along," Tony mumbled. "Have to go, Jazz. Carol-ee is getting too quiet over there in the corner."

The connection went dead; Lt. Cobb went ballistic. "I told you to get him calmed down," he yelled, "not arrange a publicity party for him! Damn it, Jazz, can't you do anything like you're told?"

"I talked to him, Vern, just like you asked. Nothing will calm him down in his condition. You know that as well as I do."

Detective Smits said, "Guys, guys. If anything, we're supposed to be getting the hostage out, not sending more in."

Lt. Cobb's eyes burned holes in Malone. "Hand it to bonehead here to screw things up."

Detective Smits turned to the table and spoke briefly on the phone, then called the Tactical C.O. over. When they were done talking, the C.O. radioed for four sharpshooters. He ordered them to suit-up in full body armor.

When they arrived, two shooters headed immediately for the front door of Tony's office, the other two went around the rear corridor. Noise in the waiting room had dropped to almost nothing.

"For the record, Jazz, you go in at your own risk," Detective Smits said. "Our shooters are at the doors, but once inside, you're on your own."

"Where's Donna Preston?" Malone said. "Tony specifically asked for her."

Lt. Cobb motioned toward the doorway.

26

Dressed in a black, two-piece suit with a red scarf knotted at her neck, Channel 8's top female reporter touched a comb at her blond hair in a mirror. A makeup artist powdered her face, then dashed her eyebrows with an eyebrow pencil.

"I'm Donna Preston," she gushed, green eyes glittering and hand outstretched as she rushed over. Bent slightly at the waist, she carried a tripod stand in one hand and juggled a large video camera in the other. An accessory bag was slung on her back.

"This is so exciting. It's really a privilege to be here...."

"We know who you are, Donna, so cut the crap," Lt. Cobb snapped. "We hate to see you get shot up, so put this on."

"Well, hello to you, too, Lt. Cobb," Donna Preston huffed. She was still griping as she put everything down and donned the bulletproof vest.

Detective Smits raised a hand for silence. He looked unhappy with the way things were progressing.

"Here's how it's going to work," he said. "Once you two are inside, if we hear even one shot, we're breaking down the doors and coming in loaded for bear. Any questions?"

When nobody spoke, Smits quietly led Donna

Preston, Malone, and Cobb down the hall toward Tony's office. Threading between SWAT team members stationed at intervals between artwork, and statuary along the muted-light hallway, Smits paused at the door and put a finger to his lips, then pointed first at Malone, then at Donna, numbering them one and two. His eyes widened when he saw Anne standing behind Lt. Cobb. He shook his head vigorously and pointed her toward the waiting room.

Anne shook her head, pointed at herself, then at Tony's office. Planting both hands on her hips, she glared at Detective Smits. Cobb wagged a finger at her but Anne crossed her arms, looking even more determined.

Detective Smits frowned and Cobb looked exasperated. Knowing it was too late to go back and regroup, Smits' shoulders sagged before he gave the okay sign.

The armored SWAT members manned each side of the door, then Cobb and Smits took up positions behind them.

Malone opened the door slowly and stuck his head in.

Tony launched into a slurry version of "Send In the Clowns." The gun was on the desk beside him.

Donna Preston pushed past Malone and barged in. She began setting up her camera as if inter-viewing killers on the loose was an everyday event.

Anne held Malone's hand, and with Redford at their side they stepped in. Someone outside closed the door quickly and quietly behind them.

"Well, hey there, Donna Preston," Tony said. "You, too, Jazz…and Reddy, old boy."

He paused then, as if stunned. His words seemed to

stick in his mouth, and his eyes wandered for a moment.

"Ah, yes... and the young, sacramental virgin... back from the dead. Isn't this just too cool."

His voice suddenly deepened, "Oh, sacred priests of Quetzalcoatl! Let the royal ceremonies begin!"

The dimly lit room reeked of alcohol, sweat, and fear. Carol Martin cried quietly as she sat cowering in the corner. Welts covered her face, her hair was matted with perspiration, and her cheeks were streaked with blood and mascara.

Redford pulled hard at his leash. When Malone let go of it, he sniffed his way to where Tony sat, the gun looming large and dangerous by his hand. Malone pulled Anne away from the door and sat on the couch, hoping they would be ignored for the time being. After Tony patted him a couple times, Reddy came over and lay on the carpet by Malone's feet, relaxed but alert.

Donna turned on the camera, its bulb filling the room with a bizarre chiaroscuro of patterns. Coming around in front of the lens and holding a microphone plugged into the camera, she began speaking in a clear, firm voice.

"This is Donna Preston reporting to you, live from the beautiful Compton Towers in downtown Tampa. We're here tonight talking with Anthony Amato, a junior partner at one of Tampa Bay's most prestigious law firms, Baxter, Brannon, Moss and Amato. With us are...."

Tony scowled, then picked up the gun and pointed it at her.

"Shut the fuck up, Donna. Get your ass over here and sit down, before I knock you down."

Donna looked shocked, but recovered quickly.

"Well, okay. I...I guess I can do this on the fly."

She slipped a small plastic stand out of her accessory bag, inserted the microphone in it, then plopped down in the chair next to Tony's desk. Placing the microphone between them, she leaned in toward Tony, getting cozy.

"Mr. Amato," she began. "Our sources tell us that...."

Tony pressed the gun against her nose.

"Shut-up, Donna. Just shut-up and let me tell you and all those fine folks out there in la-la land a story."

Donna gasped and sat back, then made like she was zipping her lip. The way she was fidgeting, it wouldn't last long. Tony played with the gun, getting more agitated by the minute.

"Once upon a time, there was a very rich American who lived in Columbia. One day, he brought his lovely wife and beautiful daughter back to this great country, and they all became average, everyday ordinary citizens."

Tony stood up, the bottle in one hand, the gun in the other. Moving around the room unsteadily, he talked and waved the gun around, pointing it at each of them as he passed, and taking hits off the bottle.

"Mr. Citizen went and hired himself Mr. Lawyer, who was a young, up-and-coming partner with the best law firm in Florida. Over the years, Mr. Lawyer helped Mr. Citizen buy a bunch of stuff. A bank, an antique business, a car dealership, an orthopedic supply company, a janitorial service—and, a fine restaurant."

Falling on the couch next to Anne, Tony put his arm around her shoulders and nuzzled her with the gun. Donna rose and turned the camera in their direction, then sat down.

"But, you see, Mr. Citizen was hiding something from Mr. Lawyer. Something Mr. Lawyer should have known before he helped buy all those businesses. Mr. Citizen was funneling drug money through them all! Mr. Citizen was transferring millions and millions of nice, laundered money through his own bank back to Columbia, so the gang down there could send more and more hidden shipments of cocaine to his new country!"

Tony started back to his desk and Donna Preston stood up abruptly. With Tony staggering toward her, she moved toward the camera again, intending to turn it back on Tony.

Tony screamed and smashed her across the head with the gun. She slumped to the floor unconscious and blood gushed from her temple. His eyes bulged and he put the gun against her neck, pressing it deep into her flesh.

"I told you to fucking sit down, bitch! I'm sick of women like you, always trying to take charge, always lying about people for a big story! Fuck!"

Anne shrugged off her vest and rushed to Donna's side. Kneeling, she cradled her head, trying to stem the flow of blood with the lower edges of her blouse.

Redford jumped to attention and growled. He had his ears laid back and advanced toward Tony with his teeth bared.

"No, Anne! Don't!" Malone shouted. Everything was spiraling out of control in a matter of seconds.

He grabbed at Reddy's leash and missed. His shoulder bumped the camera and spun it around, and the bulb began strobing uncontrollably.

Tony went berserk, screaming and punching the gun at Donna's head and neck, looking ethereal in the stuttering light. He straightened and spun around when Malone moved toward him, then stuck the gun on Malone's chest. His jaw was locked tight, his face, a brutal mask.

Redford leaped and bit down on Tony's arm. Malone grabbed at the gun and at Tony as he flailed about.

Tony cursed horribly at Reddy, trying to get him to let go. He crashed the bottle on Reddy's head, sending shards of glass flying.

With Redford's jaw locked on Tony's wrist, Malone rushed him. When Tony stumbled back and fell, the gun went off.

Both doors to Tony's office came crashing in, and the room was filled in an instant with SWAT team members. All had automatic weapons trained on Tony, screaming at him to drop the gun and get on the floor.

When Malone yanked at Reddy's leash, he opened his jaw, releasing Tony's wrist. Malone turned around to Anne.

She was lying on the floor, blood pouring from a hole at the center of her chest.

He looked back at Tony. He had raised the gun as if he were about to shoot. Before he could level it, the armor-clad police officers fired simultaneously, killing him instantly.

"Get an ambulance!" Malone screamed, dropping to the floor at Anne's side.

She was breathing raggedly and her face was drained and thin. He pressed his hand over the wound and put his ear close when he heard her trying to speak.

Redford licked gently at her face. Malone tried to push him away, but he wouldn't move, and started howling a long and mournful sound.

"Help is coming Anne," Malone cried. "Please, hang on."

"Is…it my…turn…to jump?" she whispered.

Her breath flowed like a lover's sigh from between pale lips. The lovely golden lights in her eyes dimmed, the pulse at her neck faded, and she was gone.

The next afternoon, after hours of gazing at photographs of her, Malone sat staring at the darkened television. Wanting to distract himself somehow from his sorrow, he groped for the remote. Like most televisions, the sound came on before the picture.

The first words out of the speaker were, "Wherever you go, I will always be right there with you…." As the program, 'Touched by an Angel,' progressed, he heard the words, "Blessed are the mournful, for they shall be comforted."

The Creator may have been working in a mysterious and interminable way by bringing him Anne's message. But Malone felt nothing but darkness.

Three weeks passed before Malone stopped crying each night in the lonely, echoing darkness of his bedroom. Redford had taken to sleeping on the bed with him. Restless, the boy mourned Anne's absence in his own silent and stoic way.

Four months later Malone still heard her voice on crowded street corners or in a store. He would catch glimpses of her, walking along the sidewalk, stopping to play with a flush-faced child riding on a tricycle. Then she was over there, admiring a flowerbed overflowing with red and white impatiens. He would run to catch her, but she would disappear into the corners or shadows, before he could whisper that he loved her.

Everything assumed a different light one afternoon when he visited Anne's grave. He brushed away the leaves scattered across the glistening black slab, then poured fresh water in the vial holding the one red rose he left for her every week.

A female cardinal landed on a blooming gardenia bush nearby. Tilting her head this way and that, she fluttered from one branch to another, whistling and chirping, fanning her wings in an extraordinary way.

Suddenly she flew up into a large oak off to one side, then glided back, this time accompanied by one of her babies, just learning to fly. She repeated the round trips until she had three of them, trembling and complaining, perched among the branches and flowers of the gardenia. Again, she fanned her wings, this time over the babies' heads, and they all took off in different directions, twirping and chitting joyfully. They were happy it seemed, in their newfound freedom.

A few minutes later she came back. She swooped low over Malone's head, lower over Anne's gravesite, and disappeared into a stand of laurel oaks crowding the cemetery.

He and Anne had had many a late-night discussion, about life, about death, about the hereafter. She would quote some of the great philosophers, and they would argue the pros and cons of reincarnation, and how it fit so simply into the Creator's scheme of things.

Whether it was his upbringing or something else, something less predictable, Malone knew unalterably that life was unending. Anne was soaring, playful and immortal, with the angels and the cardinals. And, tomorrow, the sun would shine on a new day.

Epilogue

At Anne's funeral, a dark, rainy day in December, John Tanner showed no remorse, nor did he exhibit any emotions during the federal trial that followed. He eventually was convicted, and consigned to the federal penitentiary for the remainder of his life, with no possibility of parole.

Malone watched the television news reports about Tanner in the weeks leading up to his trial. He followed the *St. Petersburg Times'* comprehensive reporting after the trial on Tanner's unfolding web of illicit dealings.

Before Tanner's arrest, Daryl McFarland's men, listening in on an FBI phone tap, were alerted to a shipment of cocaine hidden inside three containers of spinach and peas at the Port of Tampa. They waited, allowing the shipment to be delivered to Southwestern Florida Agro Products in Oldsmar.

Hours after Tanner's arrest, Lt. Cobb and the Pinellas County medical examiner accompanied a Hillsboro County deputy to SWEFAP's Oldsmar facility with a warrant to search for Mrs. Hunter's body. DEA and FBI agents were already there and had discovered five tons of cocaine concealed inside shipping containers of frozen vegetables.

They then raided Tanner's janitorial service and discovered a hidden vault. When they opened it, they found over a quarter million dollars in cash, as well as crates filled with tear gas grenades.

Elsewhere, they found a vast array of weaponry, including 20 pounds of C-4 plastic explosive, 10 assault rifles, 14 Uzi's, and various revolvers and pistols. A week passed, then agents seized $138.4 million, spread between accounts in Tanner's bank and four others around the country, nine others around the world.

After agents seized Tanner's home and various properties, Lt. Cobb told Malone they took over a half million in cash, jewelry worth $300,000, six cars, eight mobile phones, and countless beepers. But it was Tanner's personal computers, containing his files detailing his drug transactions, Cobb had said, they wanted most of all.

Upon examining the computer files, specialists found evidence showing that Tanner had collected some $70 million in drug money over a one-year period, transferring $30 million to his Cali cartel boss in South America. Tanner also had a separate payroll for more than 50 people in the Tampa Bay area alone that were not associated in any way with his businesses. A Mafia of sorts.

McFarland's boss, Assistant Director Mitchell, believed Tanner's operation was responsible for 31 vegetable shipments, disguising over 55 tons of cocaine. He noted that since the Columbian government does not allow extradition of its citizens, so many of Tanner's cartel connections would remain free and likely never come to trial.

One year later, Malone learned the Mayan sacrificial, black-jade dagger had been returned to Guatemalan authorities. They immediately turned it over to an archaeological team from the University of

Guatemala City for research and examination.

One hot, Sunday afternoon in July, it was reported that the dagger had mysteriously disappeared from its storage vault in Guatemala City. Antique dealers worldwide were informed of its existence and its historical and cultural value to the Mayan peoples. Despite on-going lengthy and protracted investigations, the priceless, one-of-a-kind dagger was never found.

After Tanner's trial, the medical examiner said in court that the new evidence—Esther Hunter's body— proved Anthony Amato's guilt. One of the most brilliant legal minds in the history of Tampa Bay, using an ancient, black jade dagger, had sacrificed Mrs. Hunter by cutting out her heart.

Carpe Diem

You may contact the author at:

fwc@frankwaltersclark.com